MISCHIEF AT MIDNIGHT

Suddenly there was an enormous flash of lightning. For the first time the Mystery Club could see the figure clearly.

'It's the same man,' Holly said excitedly.

'Wow!' Tracy exclaimed under her breath.

The figure rose again and darted swiftly across the meadow towards the Bensons' garden.

Just then there was a gigantic flash of lightning and a tremendous crack above their heads. The girls looked up. The lightning had struck a great branch of the oak tree. Sparks and flames lit up the stormy sky and a panicked flock of birds flew screeching into the night.

The girls looked on in horror as the branch began to fall . . .

The Mystery Club series

1 Secret Clues
2 Double Danger
3 The Forbidden Island
4 Mischief at Midnight
5 Dangerous Tricks
6 Missing!

Mischief at Midnight
The Mystery Club 4

Fiona Kelly

KNIGHT BOOKS
Hodder and Stoughton

Created by Ben M. Baglio
London W12 7HG

First published in Great Britain in 1993 by Knight Books

Special thanks to Sue Welford for all her help.

A Catalogue record for this book is available from the British Library

ISBN 0 340 58870 5

1 2 3 4 5 6 7 8 9 10

Printed and bound in Great Britain for Hodder and Stoughton Children's Books, a division of Hodder and Stoughton Ltd, Mill Road, Dunton Green, Sevenoaks, Kent TN13 2YA (Editorial Office: 47 Bedford Square, London WC1B 3DP) by Cox & Wyman Ltd, Reading, Berks. Typeset by Hewer Text Composition Services, Edinburgh. Printed by Cox & Wyman Ltd, Reading, Berks.

To Elise Howard,
honorary member of The Mystery Club

1 *A puzzling encounter*

'What a gorgeous old cottage!' Holly Adams, a tall, willowy girl of fifteen, remarked as the car drew up outside the last house in Goldenwood Lane.

Holly and her companion, Mrs Davies, a member of the Women's Volunteer Service, sat looking at the picturesque cottage. It was built of old York stone, with a slate roof and small, curtained windows. The large garden was bright with old-fashioned flowers and shrubs.

'Yes,' Mrs Davies replied, turning to smile at Holly. 'The old couple, Mr and Mrs Benson, moved in a year or so ago.' She lowered her voice. 'Actually, the cottage is supposed to be haunted.'

Holly grinned, her intelligent grey eyes sparkling. 'You're kidding!' she exclaimed.

Mrs Davies shrugged. 'It's only a story, of course. When I visit them, Mr Benson always teases me about it. I think he quite frightens his wife with tales of strange noises and cold draughts, poor woman.'

'Well,' Holly said enthusiastically. 'I love ghost stories. I'll have to get Mr Benson to tell me all about it.'

'You might have a job even getting them to answer the door, I'm afraid,' Mrs Davies remarked, her voice full of regret. 'They're rather reluctant to open it to strangers these days.'

'Oh?' Holly said. 'Why's that?'

'I'm not really sure. They used to be extremely friendly but they've grown rather suspicious lately. I did ask them last week if anything was wrong but they insisted they were all right. To be honest, it's all rather mysterious.'

Holly's ears pricked up. There was nothing she liked better than a good mystery.

'Maybe you could get them to talk to you,' Mrs Davies was saying. 'Tell you what they're so scared of. They used to be such a sociable old couple.'

'What happens if they won't let me in?'

Mrs Davies smiled again. 'Don't worry, Holly. I'll stay here until I see them answer the door. Or would you like me to come in with you as it's your first visit?'

Holly opened the car door. 'No, it's OK, thanks. I'm sure they'll see I'm only delivering their lunch.' She grinned confidently. 'You'll pick me up in half an hour?'

'Yes. Thanks, Holly. I'm pleased you offered to

help me out today. With two volunteers off sick, we're very short staffed.'

'I should really have helped you out before but I've been very busy,' Holly explained.

'Well, I'm grateful,' Mrs Davies replied.

Holly went round to the rear of the car and took two warm plates of roast beef and Yorkshire pudding from the heated trolley. She waved to Mrs Davies then opened the rustic garden gate and marched up the front path.

She knocked smartly on the blue painted front door. 'Meals on wheels,' she called.

When there was no reply. Holly knocked again. The curtains were closed, so she wasn't able to peer through the window to see if anyone was inside. She stared up at the first floor. The curtains were drawn across the bedroom windows too. Holly began to wonder if the Bensons were home at all!

How strange, Holly said to herself. *Either they've gone out or they really are too scared to open the door.*

Just then the curtains parted slightly and she could see someone peeping furtively through the crack.

'Meals on wheels,' Holly called again loudly. 'I've brought your lunch.'

The curtains were drawn together again.

To Holly's relief she heard the sound of the door chain being unfastened and a bolt being drawn back. The door opened to reveal a short, elderly woman, white hair like candyfloss round her head. She peered at Holly suspiciously.

'Mrs Benson?' Holly enquired.

The elderly woman nodded. 'Yes.'

'I've brought your lunch, Mrs Benson,' Holly said brightly. 'It'll go cold soon.'

'You're not the usual person,' the woman said, frowning. 'Where's Mrs Davies?'

'I'm helping out today.' Holly turned her head slightly to indicate Mrs Davies waiting by the kerb. 'My name is Holly Adams. Mrs Davies is in the car. She's going to deliver a few other meals along the lane.'

The old lady peered at the car then called over her shoulder. 'It's all right, Arthur. It's only lunch.' She seemed to relax. She smiled uncertainly, then stood back for Holly to step inside. 'I'm sorry,' she said. 'We don't have many visitors and we're very wary of letting any strangers in at the moment.'

'You're very wise,' Holly said. 'There are a lot of crooks and con men around these days.'

Behind her, Holly heard Mrs Benson lock and chain the door once more.

'Would you like to wait in the lounge while we eat our lunch?' Mrs Benson asked, taking the tray from Holly's hands.

'Yes, if that's OK. Mrs Davies won't be back for a while.'

Mrs Benson took the tray into the kitchen, then returned. She ushered Holly into the sitting-room.

'Thanks.' Holly sat down on the old, comfortable sofa. On the small oak coffee table there were a couple of magazines and a photograph album.

'Is it OK if I look at your photographs?' Holly asked. 'I love looking at people's pictures.'

'If you like,' Mrs Benson said. 'I'm afraid they're mostly of the cottage. A bit boring for a young person like yourself.'

As she waited for the Bensons to eat their lunch, Holly glanced through the album. There were pictures of the cottage and its lovely garden. There was one of an elderly man with a wheelbarrow whom Holly assumed to be Mr Benson himself.

On the first pages of the album were several pictures of a much younger man with short, fair hair. He was tall and bronzed and was dressed in jeans and a college sweatshirt. Holly could see he bore a distinct likeness to Mrs Benson.

Holly glanced around the room. It was small and cosy, with dark oak beams criss-crossing the ceiling. On the mantelpiece, in a cardboard mount, was another photograph of the young man. This time he was standing in front of the Parthenon in Athens. The sun was blazing down. The man wore a backpack and was grinning broadly at the camera.

Holly thumbed through the rest of the album then glanced at the magazines.

Mrs Benson came into the room with her husband.

'This is Holly Adams,' Mrs Benson said by way of introduction. 'She's helping the Volunteer Service.'

Holly stood up. 'Hello, Mr Benson,' she said shaking his hand. 'Thanks for letting me see your photos. They're great. Is that your son?' Holly indicated the photo on the mantelpiece.

Holly was puzzled at the swift, secretive glance that passed between Mrs Benson and her husband.

'Er . . . yes, dear,' Mrs Benson answered. 'A friend must have taken the picture while he was on holiday. It just arrived out of the blue after – ' She broke off.

'After what?' Holly asked curiously.

'Just after he went away.' Mr Benson took the album from Holly and put it away in a drawer.

'He doesn't live here then?'

Mrs Benson shook her head. 'No.'

Mr Benson sat down stiffly in his chair by the inglenook fireplace.

'Where does – ' Holly began.

'He lives away,' Mr Benson interrupted sharply with a frown.

'What school do you go to, dear?' Mrs Benson asked, clearly wanting to change the subject.

'Winifred Bowen-Davies,' Holly answered. Her curiosity was immediately aroused. Holly was mad about mysteries of any kind and the Bensons' apparent reluctance to talk about their son seemed very odd. Most elderly people she knew were all too happy to talk about their children. Maybe they had quarrelled about something.

'Where do you live, Holly?' Mr Benson was asking.

Holly told the old couple about her family's four-bedroomed cottage, located where the old and the new parts of Willow Dale met.

'We're renovating it,' she explained. 'But I'm afraid it's taking ages. We always seem to be in a mess. We lived in Highgate before we moved here.'

'How long have you lived in Willow Dale?' Mrs Benson asked.

'Not all that long. My mum's a bank manager and she was transferred to one of the banks in town.'

'Do you like it here?' the old woman asked.

'Oh, yes!' Holly replied enthusiastically. 'I do now.'

Holly thought about her rather lonely and unhappy first weeks in the picturesque Yorkshire town of Willow Dale. She had missed her friends in Highgate, especially Peter Hamilton and Miranda

Hunt, to whom she still wrote regularly. Holly had found it difficult to fit in at her new school until she hit upon the idea of forming the Mystery Club. Since then, Holly's life had changed dramatically. The two other members of the club, Tracy Foster and Belinda Hayes, had become Holly's best friends.

The three Mystery Club members were an unlikely trio. Holly was bright and energetic with a passion for mystery novels and a burning ambition to become a journalist. Tracy, who had moved to England from California with her mother three years earlier when her parents divorced, was sporty and competitive as well as a talented musician. Belinda, the third member, was easy-going and mad about horses, food and television. She had a keen analytical mind and had proved a great asset to the club.

The original purpose of the Mystery Club was to discuss mystery novels. But to Holly's amazement, the girls soon found themselves at the centre of several real-life mysteries. And she had a strange feeling that another might be just beginning.

'We've lived in Willow Dale all our lives,' Mrs Benson was explaining. 'In fact David was born in the local hospital. He – '

Holly saw Mr Benson frown as his wife mentioned their son.

'But we only bought this cottage a year or so ago,' he interrupted quickly. 'We love it here. It's so peaceful. Or, it was until . . . '

Holly waited a minute for the old man to go on. 'Until what, Mr Benson? Has something happened to upset you?'

Mr Benson shook his head. 'No . . . no, of course not.'

'Mrs Davies told me the cottage is supposed to be haunted,' Holly said.

Holly saw Mrs Benson glance nervously at her husband. Maybe that was it. Maybe the old couple had been frightened by the ghost.

But to Holly's surprise a grin spread across Mr Benson's face. 'Now come on, June, you know it's only a story.' He looked at Holly. 'My wife believes in that sort of thing,' he added.

'You make me worse with all those stories you tell,' Mrs Benson said with a small smile.

'Well, you have to admit that room's always cold.'

'That's because it doesn't get any sun.' Mrs Benson turned to Holly. 'He really does make me nervous sometimes. It's bad enough as things are, without his stories to make it worse.'

'Make what worse?' Holly asked quickly.

'Nothing.' Mr Benson rose stiffly from his chair. 'Would you like to see the haunted room?'

'Oh, yes, please!'

'Come on then.' Mr Benson smiled. 'You wash up, Mother,' he said to his wife.

'Oh, I'm sure that's not necessary,' Holly said. 'We can do that for you.'

Mrs Benson shook her head. 'No indeed,' she insisted. 'If you people are good enough to bring us a meal then the least I can do is wash the dishes. After all I'm not helpless.'

'And I'll show Holly the haunted room,' Mr Benson said.

Just at that moment there was a loud knock at the front door.

Holly saw Mrs Benson jump. Her hand flew to her mouth. 'Who can that be?' she exclaimed. It was clear the knock had scared her out of her wits.

Holly moved the curtain aside and looked out of the window. A tall, elegant woman with long dark hair and pale skin was standing on the doorstep, a letter in her hand. She wore a fashionable red suit with black high-heeled shoes. She was tapping her foot impatiently.

'It's a woman,' Holly said. 'She's got a letter for you by the looks of it.' She turned to see the old couple hurrying out of the room.

'Could you go please, Holly?' Mr Benson said over his shoulder. 'Tell her we're having our lunch.'

Before Holly could argue, the loud knock came again.

Holly hurried down the hall. She took the chain off the door and unlocked it.

On the doorstep, the smart woman looked startled for a moment. Then she smiled.

'Hello, dear. Can I possibly see Mr Benson, please?'

Although the woman was polite, Holly could see she was bristling with impatience.

'I'm afraid he's eating his lunch,' Holly said.

The woman stepped forward as if to push past. Holly stood her ground, putting her arm on the door frame to bar the woman's entrance.

'Perhaps I could give him a message?' she said firmly.

'I'm sorry, dear,' the woman said, 'but I really must see him. It's very important.' She smiled again. Her crimson lipstick was like a gash of blood across her face. 'Excuse me.'

Holly had no choice but to step back to allow her to pass.

'Hey!' Her protest came too late. The woman, seeing the front room empty, had disappeared into the kitchen. There, Holly heard voices.

'Well, here it is, Mr Benson. It's all in writing.'

Holly couldn't make out Mr Benson's reply.

Entering the kitchen, Holly saw the woman give Mr Benson the envelope.

'I warn you though,' the woman went on. 'We intend to take action if you don't comply with our wishes. I'd really like to prevent that if at all possible. I hate the thought of you and Mrs Benson being upset.'

'I've already given you my answer,' Mr Benson replied.

'Oh, come on,' the woman said in the same wheedling tone. Her dark eyes glittered. 'Surely you can see the sense in it?'

'No,' Mr Benson said emphatically. 'We don't see any sense in it. Now please leave.'

The woman shrugged. 'OK. But don't say I didn't warn you. Things could get very nasty if – '

'Just go!' Mr Benson shouted. Holly could see he was shaking with anger. Mrs Benson stood behind him, white-faced.

The woman shrugged. 'Very well,' she said icily. She spun on her heel and marched out.

Holly followed her to the front door.

'Thank you so much.' The woman looked Holly up and down. She frowned, her dark eyebrows almost meeting in the middle. 'You're not a relation of theirs, are you?' she asked.

'No – I'm working for the Volunteer Service.'

The woman raised her eyebrows. 'Pity. You might have persuaded them to see sense.' Then she turned and made off down the path. Holly watched her slam the garden gate and walk off down the lane, high heels clicking like castanets.

Holly shut the front door and went back into the kitchen. The Bensons were arguing.

'It's no good, Arthur,' Mrs Benson was saying. She was sitting at the kitchen table, her head in her hands. 'We'll have to do as she says.'

'Never!' Mr Benson said firmly. 'She can threaten us as much as she likes but we're not going to budge!'

'But, Arthur!' Mrs Benson looked up at her husband.

Mr Benson shook his head vehemently. 'No. You can say what you like, June, but we won't give in. I want to hear no more about it.'

Mrs Benson shrugged. 'You're just a stubborn old fool, Arthur. All I can say is that we might live to regret it.' She sighed. 'I do wish David was here. He'd sort things out for us.'

Mr Benson snorted. 'No chance of that!' he said bitterly.

'Is there anything I can do to help?' Holly asked.

The Bensons looked up, startled. Mr Benson shook his head. 'No, dear.' He put the letter on the mantelpiece. Holly noticed the envelope had some kind of logo on the flap. It looked like the initials of some company or other. Mr Benson obviously wasn't going to open it while Holly was there. 'It's just a minor difference of opinion,' he assured her.

'Minor . . . ' Mrs Benson began, but she stopped when her husband frowned at her.

'Are you sure I can't help?' Holly said, sensing Mr Benson wasn't telling the truth.

Mrs Benson sniffed and managed a smile. She took out a lace-edged handkerchief and wiped her eyes. 'Yes, dear, quite sure. Let Arthur show you that wretched room before you go. I'll wash these plates up.' She stood and walked towards the sink.

Just then the sound of a car horn came from outside.

'Oh dear,' Holly exclaimed. She glanced out of the window. 'It's Mrs Davies. She must have finished delivering her meals. Can I come back another time to hear the story?'

'Of course, dear. Come whenever you like. We like having young people around.'

'I'm sorry I didn't manage to stop that woman coming in. I could see she upset you and Mrs Benson.'

Mr Benson shook his head. 'It's nothing, really.'

'Well, it didn't look like nothing,' Holly said emphatically. 'Look, I'll leave you my phone number in case you need help.' She wrote her number down on a pad by the telephone in the hall.

Whatever was wrong, Holly knew she wouldn't rest until she had got to the bottom of it. It looked as if a meeting of the Mystery Club was definitely called for!

2 *Mysterious beginnings*

'And is that all he said?'

Belinda Hayes plonked herself down on the patchwork quilt that covered Holly's bed. She lay back on the pillow and took off her wire-framed glasses. Outside, Holly's eleven year old brother Jamie was kicking his football against the wall of the house.

Belinda's figure was reflected in Holly's full-length pine mirror. As usual, her dark brown hair was untidy and her old green sweatshirt and jeans looked as if they needed a good wash. She rubbed one eye then replaced her spectacles, blinking like an owl.

'Yup.' Holly looked up from the red Mystery Club notebook. 'He said it was just a small difference of opinion.'

Tracy Foster snorted. Her usually smiling face and bright blue eyes looked serious. 'That woman sounds awful.' She ran her hand through her short blonde hair.

'Well . . . ' Holly said. 'She seemed OK at first.

I mean she was polite enough. Quite friendly even. Called me "dear" and everything. But I got the feeling that underneath she had a heart of stone.'

'Sounds like my mother,' Belinda interjected. Belinda's disagreements with her snobbish mother were a constant source of amusement for the Mystery Club.

The others grinned.

'And the old man didn't even read the letter?' Tracy asked.

Holly shook her head. 'No . . . not when I was there anyway.'

'Well,' Tracy went on, 'it sure sounds more than a small difference of opinion to me. Who on earth was she anyway?' Her voice still held a hint of an American accent, especially when her temper was aroused.

'I don't know.' Holly shrugged. She tucked her light brown hair behind her ear. 'She didn't give me her name or anything.'

'Dracula's Bride?' Belinda suggested. She unwrapped a Mars bar and took a bite.

'Belinda, are you going to take this seriously or not?' Holly said.

Her friend waved a hand in the air. 'Sorry. Go on . . . '

Holly shrugged again. 'Well, that's all, really. 'Oh, yes . . . ' She went on to tell the others about the Bensons' son. 'That was another strange thing,' she concluded.

'I expect they've fallen out about something,' Belinda commented.

Holly shook her head. 'No, it was more than that. I'm sure.'

'Well, it doesn't sound like much of a mystery to me, Holly,' said Belinda. 'I mean, Mrs Dracula could be the old couple's landlady. Maybe they owe her rent. If so, it's not really any of our business, is it?'

Holly shook her head. 'No. They own the cottage, they told me. It was definitely more than that. There was something really sinister about that woman. She's obviously threatening them and I want to know why.'

Belinda stood up. 'Well, I must go and feed Meltdown. He'll be kicking his stable to bits and my mother will be worrying in case the neighbours complain about the noise.' She tried to rub a speck of chocolate from the knee of her jeans. 'What's our next move with the Bensons then, Miss Junior Agatha Christie?'

Holly looked thoughtful. 'Let's all go and see them. Mr Benson said he would tell me about the haunted room, so that can be our excuse. I can say you two are dying to hear about the ghost.'

'Aren't you going to deliver their meals any more then?' Belinda asked.

Holly shook her head. 'Mrs Davies doesn't need me for a while. She called to say her two other volunteers have started work again. But I'm sure it would still be OK to visit the Bensons.'

'Wow!' Tracy grinned. 'Mrs Dracula and a haunted room! This is going to be really exciting!' She picked up one of Holly's sweatshirts and draped it over her face and head, waving her arms around dramatically. 'Whooo . . . I am the ghost of Goldenwood Lane!'

Suddenly, from outside, a loud screech pierced the early evening air. 'Ooh!' Tracy stopped dead in her tracks, wrenching the sweatshirt off her head. 'What was that?'

Holly collapsed on the bed laughing. 'The ghost of Adams Cottage,' she said in a spooky voice.

'No, really . . . '

Holly laughed again. 'It was only my father's band-saw in his workshop. He's sawing up some wood to make a table.'

Tracy threw the sweatshirt at Holly. 'Very funny! It really scared me for a minute.'

'You've been watching too many horror movies,' Belinda remarked.

'Now when do I have time to watch movies?' Tracy replied, smiling as usual.

'Well, you are so incredibly well organised,' Belinda said, pretending to be sarcastic. 'What with all your sports clubs, aerobics, orchestra rehearsals and the occasional date with Kurt Welford, I thought you'd easily fit in visits to the cinema as well.' She sighed. 'It makes me tired just thinking about it.'

'Come on, you two,' Holly said. 'When shall we go to Goldenwood Lane?'

'Tomorrow?' Tracy suggested. 'I've got tennis practice in the morning but after that I'm free. How about you, Belinda?'

'I'm always free.' Belinda grinned. 'Except when I'm riding Meltdown, of course. Tomorrow will be fine.'

When the girls had gone, Holly sat staring thoughtfully at a poster on her bedroom wall. She felt a surge of excitement. It was the feeling she always had whenever there was a new mystery to solve.

Holly picked up the novel that lay on her bedside table. She thumbed through the pages. *The Mystery of the Fire Emerald* it was called. She had guessed who had stolen the heroine's jewels miles before the end of the book, *and* why the man with one leg had lied to the police. Maybe one day she would be a mystery writer too. Or an investigative journalist. Holly could just imagine herself being top crime writer for the *Yorkshire Post*.

She sighed. All she did at the moment was write boring articles for *Winformation*, the school magazine. She had fallen out with the editor,

Steffie Smith, ages ago. And her latest assignment was about the most boring subject in the universe – the local Rambling and Footpath Society. Holly couldn't imagine who on earth would be interested in a subject like that! Luckily, her father had lent her a book about the local area and it was proving to be quite helpful. Maybe she could make something of the article after all.

Holly sighed again and looked at her watch. Enough time to make some more notes before supper.

Just then, the telephone rang.

Holly ran to answer it on the extension in her parents' room.

'Holly?'

It was Mrs Benson.

'Look, Holly.' The elderly lady was hardly speaking above a whisper. 'I'm very worried in case you tell anyone about that woman who visited us today.'

'Why?' Holly asked.

'Well, I'm frightened that – well, let's just say that it's no one else's business. We really don't want people talking about us.'

'I'm afraid I've already mentioned it to a couple of friends of mine,' Holly admitted.

'Oh, dear . . . ' Mrs Benson sounded scared. 'Perhaps you'd better ask them not to say anything. You see, the whole thing is tied up with – '

Mrs Benson suddenly broke off. Holly heard an angry voice in the background shouting something.

'For goodness' sake, Arthur,' Holly heard Mrs Benson say, 'I'm only talking to Holly Adams.'

Mr Benson shouted something else but Holly couldn't make out what it was.

Mrs Benson came back on the line. 'I'm sorry, dear,' she said abruptly. 'I've got to go . . . goodbye.'

'But, Mrs Benson – ' Holly began, wanting to tell the old lady of the girls' intended visit. But it was too late. The telephone had been slammed down.

Holly put the telephone down with a sigh. What on earth was going on over at Goldenwood Lane?

By the tone of Mrs Benson's scared and secretive voice it may even be a matter of life or death! Holly had a feeling the real mystery was only just beginning.

'Come *on*, you two!' Tracy stopped pedalling and waited for Holly and Belinda to catch up. The three girls were on their way to visit the Bensons the following day.

'Why do you always go so fast, Tracy?' Belinda panted, bringing up the rear as usual. It was a warm day and Belinda's face was red with exertion. She took off her glasses and rubbed them on the sleeve of her sweatshirt.

Tracy smiled. 'You'll have to join my aerobics class, Belinda. You'll soon get fit.'

'Yes,' Belinda grinned. 'Fit to drop!'

Holly pedalled on ahead. 'Well, are you coming or not, you two?'

The Mystery Club soon arrived at the Bensons' cottage on Goldenwood Lane. Beside it, Holly noticed a wide, grassy path that led to a small orchard full of apple and plum trees. Beyond that, the wild plants and flowers of the Bensons' paddock swayed in the breeze.

They parked their bikes by the front fence, went through the wooden gate and up the garden path.

'I bet they're not going to answer,' Holly said, knocking on the front door for the third time. 'I should have phoned to say we were coming.'

'They've probably gone out,' Belinda remarked, leaning across one of the flower-beds to peer into a window. As before, the floral curtains were drawn tightly shut.

'I doubt it,' Holly said. 'That's why they get their meals delivered. They have trouble getting out.'

Tracy pulled Belinda's arm. 'You'll scare them more than ever if they see your mug looking in at them.' She grinned at her friend.

'Charming!' Belinda replied good-naturedly. She pushed her straggly hair behind her ear and stepped back on to the path. 'I'll go round the back and see if they're there.'

But at the rear of the cottage there was no one in sight. Belinda leaned over the coal bunker to peer into the kitchen window. The room was empty. She walked round to the garden shed and a pretty, white-painted Victorian summer-house. She peered through the summer-house windows. Apart from a few odds and ends – a moth-eaten carpet laid on the floor, a couple of dusty deckchairs and a few wooden apple boxes – it was empty. It didn't look as if anyone had been in there for years.

Belinda walked through the damp grass of the orchard and leaned her elbows on the fence. She stared out over the meadow. Painted Lady butterflies and huge bumble-bees flew from flower to flower. There were buttercups, ox-eye daisies and tall, bronze heads of sorrel. *What lovely hay it would make for Meltdown*, Belinda thought wistfully.

Suddenly she noticed a flash of light in the wood that bordered the field. Belinda frowned. What on earth could it be? A torch? Not in broad daylight, surely. She shrugged. It was probably just kids playing.

Just as she was about to dismiss the whole incident as a product of her imagination, a figure stepped out from the trees into the sunlight. It was a man with a pair of binoculars hanging round his neck. As Belinda watched, the man seemed to notice her. He dodged quickly back into the trees. There was another flash of light as the sun's rays caught the lenses.

Belinda wondered who he could be. Why on earth was he observing the cottage so closely? She felt a pang of apprehension. It was horrible to think someone might be watching you, like something out of a spy film. Belinda had a sudden feeling that this whole affair might turn out to be even more sinister than the Mystery Club had anticipated.

Round the front, she found Holly and Tracy talking to Mr Benson on the doorstep.

The old man frowned as Belinda approached. 'Who are you?' he asked suspiciously. 'Why are you trespassing on my – '

'It's OK, Mr Benson,' Holly said hurriedly. She put a reassuring hand on his arm. 'It's our friend Belinda. When no one answered the door we thought you might be round the back. She just went to see.'

The old man looked relieved. He ran a hand through his grey hair. 'Sorry, young lady,' he said. 'I didn't realise there were three of you.'

'I'm afraid so.' Belinda smiled, held out her hand and introduced herself. 'What a lovely wood on the other side of the paddock,' she said finally. 'Are people allowed to ride horses there?'

Mr Benson nodded. 'The only access is through my land, but you're welcome to ride there any time.

There's a bridle path through the wood. Students from the riding school often come through here.'

'Great!' Belinda said enthusiastically. 'Thanks, Mr Benson.'

'I'll show you the path if you like,' Mr Benson said. 'I'll just go in and get my walking stick. Come in, Holly, and you, Tracy. I'm sure my wife will be pleased to have some pleasant visitors for a change. Especially after last night.'

'Last night?' the girls chorused.

Mr Benson nodded. 'Yes. I'll let my wife tell you while I go for a walk with Belinda.'

Holly went a little way down the garden. 'That's a pretty summer-house,' she said to Belinda, peering inside. 'Looks a bit neglected.'

Belinda held Holly's arm. 'Never mind about the summer-house,' she hissed. 'Guess what?'

'What?'

'There was a man in the wood . . . '

'So?' Holly said.

'I'm sure he was spying on the cottage.'

'Spying?' Holly frowned. 'How odd. Are you sure?'

'Well,' Belinda said uncertainly. 'Not absolutely positive but he did have a pair of binoculars and he rushed off when he saw me.'

'What did he look like?'

Belinda shook her head. 'I couldn't actually see his face but he looked tall. He had some kind of hat on. He looked awfully mysterious to me.'

Holly frowned, biting her lip. 'I wonder if he *was* spying? Keep an eye out when you go for your walk, Belinda. But be careful. I can't imagine why anyone would be spying on the Bensons, but if they are . . . it's quite possible they could be dangerous!'

3 *In the firing line*

'While you go for a walk with Mr Benson,' Holly continued, 'Tracy and I are going to try and find out what was in that letter the woman delivered while I was here yesterday.'

'Great. What are you going to do? Steal it?'

Holly grinned. 'Don't be daft, Belinda. We'll just try and get Mrs Benson to tell us, that's all. I can't go around taking people's letters, can I?'

Belinda shrugged, looking disappointed. 'I suppose not,' she said. She hurried to catch up with Mr Benson.

In the front room of the cottage Tracy was talking to Mrs Benson.

'Let me make the tea, Mrs Benson.'

'No, dear,' the old woman insisted. 'I can do it. You make yourself comfortable.'

Tracy went over to the mantelpiece and picked up the photograph of the Bensons' son. To her horror the photo slipped sideways out of its cardboard mount and fell to the floor. Tracy glanced over her shoulder guiltily then picked it up. The date the picture had been taken was printed in the bottom left hand corner, hidden before by its mount. The tenth of August the previous year, Tracy noticed. She quickly put it back in the mount and replaced it on the mantelpiece.

Just then Holly came in.

'What did Belinda have to say?' Tracy asked.

Holly told her quickly about the man with binoculars.

'That's really weird,' Tracy said, looking worried.

'I know,' Holly replied. 'I warned her to be careful.'

Out of the window Holly could see Belinda walking slowly round the edge of the field with Mr Benson. She had picked a blade of grass and was chewing it. Mr Benson was waving his arm, indicating something on the other side of the meadow.

Holly craned her neck but there was no sign of anyone watching the house. She sighed. Maybe Belinda had been mistaken.

Mrs Benson came back with a tray of tea and Tracy started to tell her about the nursery her mother ran.

'She started it three years ago,' Tracy explained. 'We came over from California when my mom and dad got divorced.'

'I expect your father misses you,' Mrs Benson said, sitting down with a sigh.

'I miss him too,' Tracy said sadly. 'But I get to go over there sometimes.'

'I know I miss my David,' Mrs Benson went on wistfully. 'That's him on the mantelpiece.'

'Yes,' Holly and Tracy chorused. They exchanged glances. Would Mrs Benson tell them more about him now she was on her own? If they could find out where David lived, they could get in touch with him. If his parents were being intimidated by that mysterious woman then he was really the right one to deal with it.

'Does he live far away, Mrs Benson?' Tracy asked, smiling casually.

'Er . . . not that far but we don't see him very often.' She glanced over her shoulder. 'Arthur doesn't like me to talk about him,' she said in a low voice.

'Why on earth not?' Tracy said.

Mrs Benson shrugged. 'Well . . . oh dear, I don't know really. I've told Arthur that lots of people have – ' She broke off.

The girls leaned forward.

Mrs Benson shrugged again. 'Oh . . . nothing. We just don't see him very often, that's all. Now, let me tell you about last night . . . '

Just then the telephone rang. Mrs Benson jumped nervously, spilling some of her tea on to her apron.

'Oh, goodness!' she exclaimed. 'I'm getting to be a nervous wreck. I wonder who that can be.' Her fingers shook as she tried to wipe the stain with a handkerchief. 'I wish Arthur was here . . . ' She looked at Holly. 'I don't suppose you could answer it for me, could you?'

Holly and Tracy exchanged another glance.

'Yes, of course.' Holly patted Mrs Benson's arm reassuringly. 'Don't worry. I'll find out who it is.'

The telephone continued to ring. Whoever it was was obviously determined to keep hanging on until someone answered.

Holly picked up the receiver. There was a click as if the person at the other end was in a call box.

'Is Mr Benson there, please?' A woman's deep voice came from the other end of the line.

Although she had only heard it once before, Holly recognised the voice immediately. The Bensons' mysterious visitor!

'No. I'm afraid he isn't. Who's calling, please?'

The caller ignored Holly's query. 'Where is he?' she asked sharply.

'I'm afraid he's gone out for a walk in the wood.' As soon as she realised what she'd said, Holly bit her lip. She shouldn't have let on where Mr Benson had gone.

'What about his wife?'

'I'm sorry,' Holly apologised, hoping to sound

sincere. 'She can't come to the phone at the moment. Can I take a message?'

The woman made an impatient sound. 'Just tell them that we really do need an answer to our letter immediately.'

'Yes, I'll tell them. Who shall I say called?'

'They'll know who I am, dear. Just say if they don't agree to our proposition, we've got some information that just might make them change their minds.'

'But – ' Holly began. But the line had gone dead.

Holly put down the receiver. She stood for a moment, fiddling with the telephone cord. Should she pass the woman's message on to the Bensons? The last thing she wanted was for them to be more upset than they were already. Maybe she could just say a woman had called but that she hadn't left any message. Surely a little white lie wouldn't hurt? Not if it saved the old couple from being upset.

Holly drew a deep breath. If the Mystery Club was to find out what was going on, she had to keep cool.

As she turned to go back into the lounge, Holly noticed a pile of letters on the shelf below the telephone. She picked them up. Feeling guilty, she glanced round, but the door was closed and Holly could hear Mrs Benson and Tracy talking.

Quickly, Holly sifted through the pile. Several

letters were postmarked somewhere in Derbyshire and were addressed in the same sloping handwriting. One or two appeared to be bills. But another couple of envelopes were printed with the same motif that Holly had seen when the woman delivered her letter to the Bensons in person.

Holly's pulse thudded excitedly. The letters bore postmarks several days before Holly's visit. So the one the woman had brought by hand wasn't the first the Bensons had received. The fact she had delivered it herself might well mean that she was getting very impatient.

Holly heard footsteps approaching. Hurriedly, she replaced the letters on the shelf.

'Who was on the phone?' Mrs Benson was standing in the doorway, looking at Holly with a worried expression. Tracy stood behind her, her hand on the old lady's shoulder.

'I'm afraid it was that woman who brought you the letter yesterday,' Holly said truthfully. 'She didn't give her name. She just said she'd ring back another time.'

'Oh, dear,' Mrs Benson said.

Holly put her arm round Mrs Benson's shoulders, walking the old woman back into the sitting-room. She sat her down on the sofa. 'Look, Mrs Benson,' she said. 'If that woman is threatening you, I really think you ought to tell the police.'

'Yes,' Tracy agreed. 'You should. I'm sure they

could do something about it. What did she say in her letter anyway?'

Mrs Benson looked scared. 'I can't tell you that, I'm afraid.'

'Can't you tell the police then?'

Mrs Benson shook her head. 'No, it's not a matter for the police. And please, both of you, don't tell Arthur she called. He'll only be angry and upset.'

Holly shrugged. 'OK, Mrs Benson, if that's what you want.' She gave the old lady a hug. 'Just promise me you'll let us know if you need any help, OK?'

Mrs Benson managed a wan smile. 'I promise,' she said, rising. 'I'll just go and fill the pot with fresh tea then I'll tell you about the strange things that happened last night.'

Holly nudged her friend. 'At last,' she said. 'I've been dying to hear what's happened ever since we arrived!'

Meanwhile, Belinda and Mr Benson had walked slowly around the long grass of the paddock and into the wood. The bridle path wound its way through a cluster of old oak and beech trees then out into a clearing. The previous year's fallen leaves still lay in a golden carpet beneath their feet.

'The riders keep the path clear of brambles,' Mr Benson explained.

Belinda could hear a blackbird singing and rooks

caw-cawing in the high branches of the oaks. Mr Benson had told her the wood had been there for centuries.

'How lovely,' Belinda said. 'I'm really looking forward to riding my horse in here. Can I really come whenever I like?'

The thought of a good gallop through the woods on her lively chestnut thoroughbred always brought a flush of enthusiasm to Belinda's cheeks.

Mr Benson nodded. 'Yes, at least this is one area where people can still enjoy the countryside. Although I don't know for how long. You know, when I was a young man, all that land on the other side of Willow Dale used to be woods and fields like this.'

'You mean where they've built the new sports centre and shopping centre?'

'That's right.' Mr Benson shook his head and looked sad. 'Soon there won't be any open spaces left.'

Looking through the trees to the edge of the wood, they could just make out a white van parked along the lane.

'I wonder who that belongs to?' Mr Benson remarked. 'It's an odd place to be parked.'

'I saw a man with binoculars earlier on,' Belinda said. 'He seemed to be watching the cottage for some reason,' she added without thinking.

'Oh, dear.' Mr Benson stopped suddenly. 'I think

we'd better go back. I don't like leaving Mrs Benson on her own for too long.'

Belinda bit her lip. The old man was obviously worried. She tried to reassure him. 'The others are with her,' she said. 'I'm sure she'll be OK.'

Just then a gunshot echoed through the wood towards them. Belinda jumped. Who on earth was shooting so close to where they were walking? As she turned towards the sound, a dark figure dodged behind a tree.

'Are people allowed to shoot in here?' Belinda asked, surprised.

Mr Benson shook his head, frowning. 'No, they're not. I can't think who it can be. I haven't seen anyone go past this morning. Unless that's their van over there. They could have climbed the fence, I suppose.'

Another shot rang out. This time Belinda could hear the high pitched whine associated with a high velocity shotgun. It sounded too close for comfort.

'I don't think we'd better hang around to find out,' Belinda said.

Through the trees she caught a glimpse of the dark figure stalking through the brambles, a shotgun held in front of him. As she watched, the figure lifted the weapon and pointed it into the trees.

Belinda took Mr Benson's arm. 'I think we'd better get back!'

A third shot rang out. They both ducked down in fright.

'Do you think he could actually be shooting at us?' she whispered. Beside her, she could feel Mr Benson shaking.

Mr Benson shook his head. 'Surely not?'

'If we keep quiet,' Belinda said sensibly, 'maybe he'll think we've gone.'

Mr Benson and Belinda crouched in the undergrowth. Belinda's heart was beating so loudly she felt sure the gunman would hear it. They heard the sound of someone crashing towards them. A flock of startled pigeons flew through the branches, their wings seeming to beat out a warning of danger.

Through the dappled sunlight. Belinda could see the figure standing close to their hiding-place, legs apart. He took a couple more cartridges from his pocket and loaded the gun. Slowly he turned and pointed the gun in their direction . . .

4 *The haunted room*

Belinda held her breath. All around, the woodland sounds seemed magnified a hundred times. Peering through her fingers, she saw the dark figure looming above. It turned this way, then that. He was definitely looking for something . . . or someone.

Belinda suddenly had an idea. She picked up a large stone and threw it as hard as she could into the distance. She heard it crash against a tree then fall into the brambles.

The figure began to run towards it, smashing through the undergrowth. Belinda saw him trip and fall headlong into the brambles. A muffled curse echoed through the woodland. He struggled to his feet and ran off.

'Quick!' Belinda pulled Mr Benson to his feet. She hurried the old man back along the bridle path as fast as he could go. Spotting a couple of spent cartridges lying in the undergrowth, she hastily bent to pick them up. She stuffed them, still warm, into the pocket of her jeans.

'Mr Benson, you've got to tell the police about this. That person must be insane!'

Mr Benson shook his head. 'No,' he said firmly. 'I'd rather we didn't.'

'But we could have been killed!' Belinda protested. 'If I had been riding through here, poor Meltdown probably would have bolted with me! And what about those pony trekkers you mentioned? They're only kids.'

Mr Benson shook his head. He brushed a few dead leaves from his jacket. 'Whoever it was has gone now,' he said. 'I'm sure it was all a mistake.'

Belinda was amazed. There was no doubt someone had tried to scare them – maybe even kill them. It seemed really irresponsible not to tell the police.

When she and Mr Benson emerged, shaken, from the woods, Belinda could see Tracy sprinting towards them.

'Are you all right?' Tracy called anxiously. 'We heard shots.'

'Some maniac was trying to scare us,' Belinda said angrily.

'Why on earth would anyone do that?' Tracy asked.

'I'm sure it was all a mistake,' Mr Benson said hurriedly. 'Just someone practising with a shotgun.' He brushed some more leaves from his clothes. 'No harm done.' He leaned heavily on his stick.

'No harm done!' Belinda burst out, looking shocked. Then she shrugged. The old man seemed determined to dismiss the whole episode as an accident. He was clearly stubborn as a mule.

Belinda held Tracy's arm as Mr Benson hurried towards the cottage.

'Tracy!' she cried. 'Someone really did try to frighten us away.'

'I believe you.' Tracy looked serious. 'But it's no use scaring the Bensons any more than they are already.' She went on to tell Belinda about the telephone call.

'That woman sounds as if she's really got it in for them. I wish we knew why.'

'Me too. And the sooner we find out, the better!'

Mrs Benson went pale when Mr Benson told her about the gunman.

'I hope he scratched himself to death,' Belinda said angrily, after she'd told them how the man had fallen into the brambles.

'I really don't know what's going to happen next.' Mrs Benson sat down and put her head in her hands. 'What with last night and now this . . . '

'What *did* happen last night?' Belinda asked impatiently.

'It's to do with the haunted room,' Holly explained. 'The Bensons heard strange noises – '

'It sounded like a spaceship taking off,' Mrs Benson interjected.

' . . . and stuff had been disturbed,' Holly went on.

'Don't forget that figure,' said Tracy.

Mr Benson gestured impatiently. 'What have you been telling these young people, June? I'm sure that was your imagination.'

'No, it wasn't, Arthur,' Mrs Benson said hotly. 'I definitely saw a pale, misty figure darting across the lawn.'

Mr Benson shook his head. 'I told you, sometimes the moon casts strange shadows when there's a low-lying mist like we had last night.'

Mrs Benson shook her head. 'You can say what you like, Arthur. I *know* what I saw.'

'Perhaps it was Mrs Dracula,' Belinda whispered in Tracy's ear.

'Could we see the room?' Holly asked. 'You did promise . . . '

'Yes, of course, dear,' Mrs Benson replied. 'We'll see what you girls make of it.'

Mrs Benson led the way. The haunted room was in the back part of the house, next to the kitchen.

'This is the oldest part of the house,' Mr Benson explained. 'A local builder renovated the front part when Mr and Mrs Wynne lived here. They were the previous owners. We don't use this back part much. David planned to use the room as his study. Some of the stuff in there belongs to him. But then – ' Mr Benson broke off, 'he didn't worry about ghosts.'

Mrs Benson opened the door. As she did so, a cold draught touched the girls' faces, kissing their skin with a feel of winter.

Behind Mrs Benson, Tracy nudged Holly. 'Watch out for Mrs Dracula,' she whispered. 'She might leap out on us – teeth bared, hungry for blood.' She giggled.

'I really hate coming in here.' A shudder passed across Mrs Benson's shoulders. 'After David went away I'd planned to use it as my sewing room but it's too cold. Made my bones ache.'

Holly, Tracy and Belinda stepped warily into the room. Holly shivered and hugged herself for warmth. Her pink T-shirt and white cycling shorts were no protection against the unexpected coolness of the room. Although the sun was shining outside, the room was as dim and chilly as a December evening.

'It *is* very cold,' she said.

'It never gets the sun,' Mr Benson explained. 'And I'm afraid these old houses soon get damp with no heating in the rooms.'

'I tried lighting a fire but it didn't make any difference,' Mrs Benson said with a shiver.

'Apparently there's an old cellar underneath,' Mr

Benson went on. 'The chimney draws cold air up from below.'

'The previous owners left some of these things.' Mrs Benson indicated some of the room's contents. 'That rug for instance. It was too old-fashioned for their new bungalow. And the bookshelves . . . '

Holly noticed several books on the floor. The contents of a sewing box were scattered around and a picture had fallen off the wall. The faded oriental rug that covered most of the floor was crumpled. Holly bent down to straighten it.

'Funny, I thought that rug was nailed down,' Mrs Benson said with a puzzled frown.

Tracy gathered up the scraps of material and put them back in the sewing box, tugging at one that had caught on a nail in the floorboards. She gave the box to Mrs Benson.

'I used to dress bridal dolls for the church bazaar,' Mrs Benson explained. 'I'm afraid my fingers are too stiff to do any sewing these days.'

'The noise seemed to be coming from in here,' Mr Benson explained. 'That's why we came down to investigate.'

'It's weird.' Holly walked round the room. The panelled walls were dark brown wood and the whole room had a dull and sad appearance. 'Really spooky.'

Mr Benson sat down in the chair by the window. He smiled, his eyes bright with humour. 'You obviously feel something in the air. Don't you think there's an atmosphere of desperation . . . ' Mr Benson lowered his voice. 'An atmosphere of death . . . '

'Arthur!' his wife protested. 'For goodness' sake. Aren't you content with frightening me silly without scaring these girls as well?'

Mr Benson shrugged. 'But it's true,' he said in a creepy voice. He shivered. 'You know it's true.' His voice was barely a whisper.

'Come off it, Mr Benson,' Tracy said hesitantly. 'You're kidding us – aren't you?'

'If I'm joking, how do you explain the eerie noise?' the old man replied. 'And all this?' He indicated the mess on the floor.

'It could be a poltergeist,' Belinda volunteered. 'They're supposed to throw things around. I saw a film about one once.'

'Maybe it was an earth tremor,' Tracy suggested. 'We had them all the time in California. Things used to fall off shelves and stuff . . . '

'Nothing was disturbed in any of the other rooms, so it couldn't have been anything like that,' Mrs Benson said.

'I told you,' Mr Benson added, a twinkle in his eye. 'It was Rebecca.'

'Rebecca!' The girls looked at one another in consternation. 'Who on earth is Rebecca?' said Holly.

Mr Benson looked at each girl in turn, his eyes wide. 'The ghost!'

5 *Ghost story*

The girls exchanged glances. Was there *really* a ghost named Rebecca haunting the Bensons' cottage?

Mrs Benson managed to smile at them. 'For goodness' sake, stop teasing the girls,' she said to her husband. 'Tell them the story if you must.'

Mr Benson settled back in the chair. 'This cottage used to be much larger, part of an old manor house that was built in the eighteenth century. This room was part of the dining hall. The whole estate belonged to a wealthy family called Smythe. Rebecca was the only child and she lived here in about 1850. She was a beautiful girl, born on New Year's day. She was the apple of her parents' eyes.'

'Just like me,' Belinda whispered with a giggle.

'Shh!' Tracy nudged her arm.

'Apparently she fell in love with a gypsy,' Mr Benson continued.

Tracy sighed. 'How romantic!'

Belinda snorted. 'Sounds a bit corny to me.'

'And her father believed the young man was after the family's wealth. He refused to let her see him . . . he even locked her up.'

'Poor thing!' Holly exclaimed.

'The legend says she refused all food and starved to death.'

'In this room?' Tracy said, her blue eyes wide with disbelief.

'No, in another room that has long since disappeared, when part of the manor burned down. But . . . ' Mr Benson's eyes twinkled. 'They used to meet secretly in this room until one day her father discovered them together.'

'Wow!' Tracy breathed.

'After her death the family line died out,' Mr Benson said. 'The ghost of Rebecca is still supposed to be waiting for her lover.'

There was silence for a moment or two whilst the girls took in the story.

'Poor thing . . . ' Holly said at last in a dreamy, faraway voice.

'What a load of rubbish,' Belinda remarked acidly. 'Fancy *starving* yourself to death!'

'Yes, of course it's all nonsense,' Mr Benson said, rising. 'But you know how country people love their folk tales.'

'There must be some rational explanation,' Holly said.

Tracy shrugged. 'I bet someone's trying to scare you, Mr and Mrs Benson.'

Holly noticed a swift glance pass between the old couple.

'It could be those youngsters from the estate,' Mr Benson said without conviction. 'I've seen a few of them hanging around. I expect someone told them the story of the ghost and they decided to give us a scare.'

Holly picked a book up off the floor. She opened it. *David Michael Benson* was written in sloping handwriting on the inside of the cover. 'Well, although I'd like to think it was poor Rebecca,' she said, 'I reckon someone *is* playing tricks on you. It might be a good idea to get locks fixed on your windows. I bet these old-fashioned windows are quite easy to force open.'

'Yes,' Mr Benson agreed. 'We will.'

'Do lots of people know about the legend?' Holly asked as the girls filed out.

'Oh, yes,' Mr Benson said, nodding. 'The last owners were quite proud of it. When David came to view the property they told him the whole story. He used to tell everyone his parents had moved into a haunted cottage. Made quite a joke of it.'

At that moment, the postman drew up outside the house. When the letters came through the door Mr Benson hurried to pick them up. He shuffled through them anxiously. Holly noticed another envelope with the same strange logo on the flap. She could examine it closely for the first time. It was two letters entwined. A capital 'S' and a capital 'H'.

'Is there one from – ' Mrs Benson broke off.

'Yes,' Mr Benson said gruffly, putting the letters on the hall table.

'She's not going to give up, you know,' his wife replied.

'My father used to be a lawyer,' Holly said. 'I'm sure he'd be able to give you advice if you needed it.'

'That might be an idea, Arthur,' Mrs Benson said enthusiastically.

Mr Benson shook his head. 'No. We don't need anyone's advice and we haven't much faith in lawyers, I'm afraid.'

'Why not?' Holly asked.

'Let's just say we've had a bad experience with them,' Mr Benson said mysteriously. 'Thank you all the same, Holly, but this dispute is our business and no one else's!'

The elderly couple stood on the doorstep to wave the girls goodbye.

A few hundred metres up the road Holly stopped pedalling. She got off her bicycle and leant it against a stone wall. 'OK, you lot,' she said, 'what did you find out? Belinda, you first.'

'All I found out,' Belinda said angrily, 'was that

some idiot tried to scare us away from that wood. Here . . . ' She took the spent cartridges from her pocket and handed them to Holly. 'I found these. They were still warm when I picked them up.'

Holly held one up. 'These are unusual.'

'How do you mean?' Tracy took one of the cartridges from Holly and examined it.

'Well,' Holly explained, 'my uncle collects old guns. He showed me a couple of cartridges like this once. I think they're homemade.'

Tracy gave the cartridge back to Holly. 'I've never seen any kind of cartridge before, so I don't know.' She shuddered. 'I hate guns. Even the starting pistol at track meets makes me jump out of my skin.'

'They're supposed to,' Belinda remarked drily.

'Anything else?' Holly asked.

Belinda shook her head ruefully. 'No. It's a pity I didn't get a good look at whoever it was. All I know is he was wearing some kind of dark jacket and trainers. Just like millions of other people.'

'Do you think it was the same man you saw with binoculars?' Holly asked.

Belinda shrugged. 'Could have been, I suppose.'

Holly was making notes in the red Mystery Club notebook. When she had finished, she put her hand on her friend's shoulder. 'I'm glad you weren't hurt.'

'Me too,' Belinda said with a wry grin. 'Who

would ride my beautiful Meltdown? And how on earth would you two ever manage without me?'

Tracy grinned and punched Belinda playfully on the arm. 'We'd be devastated, all right,' she said.

Holly smiled. Belinda always managed to keep her sense of humour whatever happened.

'Well, Holly, what else did we find out?' Tracy asked.

Holly shrugged. 'That our lovely Mrs Dracula is still harassing the old couple. By phone and letter. I saw several envelopes in the hall, all with the same company logo on.'

'What was it like?' Tracy asked.

'An S and H intertwined like this . . . ' Holly drew the logo in her notebook and showed it to the others. 'Ever seen it before?' she asked.

Tracy and Belinda shook their heads.

'Nope,' Belinda said. 'Doesn't mean a thing.'

'Then there was the haunted room,' Holly said thoughtfully, looking at her notes. 'That was really weird, all that stuff being moved about. Someone's definitely trying to frighten them.'

'You don't believe in Rebecca then?' Belinda grinned.

'I'd really like to but I'm afraid this was human, not ghostly mischief. Someone broke in and messed around with their things. I'm positive.'

'I think the first thing we should do is try to find out who that horrible woman is and where she comes from.' Tracy said.

'That makes sense,' Belinda agreed.

'. . . and what exactly it is she wants.'

'Whatever it is, she's obviously determined to get it,' Holly said. 'She might even be employing someone to put the frighteners on . . . '

'What, like the Mafia?' Belinda's eyes sparkled.

Holly grinned. 'Not quite. But there are people who'll do anything for money.'

'What I don't understand,' Tracy began, 'is what on earth the Bensons have that Mrs Dracula so desperately wants. They don't seem to be very well off or anything.'

'I can't imagine,' Belinda said. 'Unless . . . '

'Unless what?' The other two girls leaned forward eagerly.

'Unless . . . ' Belinda hesitated again, adjusting the strap of her cycling helmet, '. . . they're involved in some kind of crime ring,' she declared.

Holly giggled. 'What kind of crime ring, Belinda?'

Belinda shrugged. 'I don't know . . . accepting charity meals then selling them to neighbours at extortionate prices!'

Holly and Tracy threw back their heads and laughed.

'Your imagination's running away with you, Belinda,' Tracy said, wiping her eyes. She stopped laughing and looked serious. 'We shouldn't really joke about it.'

'No,' Holly agreed soberly. 'I'm convinced they really do need help.'

'Maybe they've got an attic full of priceless antiques and Mrs Dracula's desperate to get hold of them,' Belinda suggested.

'Well, she certainly wants something from them,' Holly said. 'She said on the phone that she's got some information that could *make* them do as she asks. I just hope we can find out what it is.'

'That sounds like blackmail to me,' Belinda commented, looking serious.

'Me too,' Tracy agreed with a grim face.

'Well, we didn't learn any more about David,' Holly said. 'I wish we knew where he was. He'd be bound to try to help. Hey . . . I've just realised – '

'What?' asked the others.

'When I answered the phone there were some letters on the hall table . . . '

'Yes?' Tracy said eagerly.

'There were several postmarked Derbyshire – and all addressed in the same handwriting,' Holly continued.

'So?'

'And one of those books I picked up in the haunted room had David Benson's name written inside.'

'And it was the same handwriting?' Tracy said excitedly.

'Right!'

'Brilliant!' Belinda exclaimed. 'Now all you have to do is sneak a look inside the envelopes and, bingo, you know where he lives.'

'I suppose he *would* want to help them,' Tracy said doubtfully. 'I mean if they've quarrelled . . . '

'It's a risk we'll have to take,' Holly said. 'The trouble is . . . ' Her voice trailed off.

'What?'

'I can't really go about reading other people's private letters.'

Belinda shrugged her shoulders. 'Well, if it's either that or never find out where David is, I know which I'd choose.'

Holly looked at Tracy. 'What do you think?'

'I think we've got to do it. There's no alternative.'

'Anyway,' said Belinda, 'Miss Marple reads other people's letters all the time.'

'No, she doesn't,' Holly said, laughing. 'She solves her mysteries by shrewd deduction and clever thinking.'

'Just like us,' Tracy said. 'Just like the Mystery Club.' She buckled her day-glo orange helmet. 'Well, buddies, who's for a race home?'

Belinda made a face. 'Not me, I'm going to ride Meltdown later. I'm saving my energy.' She took a bag of sweets from her pocket. 'Want a jelly baby?'

Tracy laughed, her blue eyes sparkling. 'No, thanks.'

'Holly?'

Holly smiled and took a sweet. 'Thanks, Belinda. I've got to get home too. I've got to finish that thrilling article about the Rambling and Footpath Society for the school magazine.'

Belinda made a face. 'It sounds horrendously boring.'

Holly shrugged. 'I only seem to get boring stuff to write about these days.'

As she spoke, a white van suddenly pulled out from the lay-by and began to head towards them.

'Hey . . .' Belinda said, stopping rapidly in her tracks. 'I've seen that van before.'

'Where?' Holly asked curiously.

'It was parked in the lane. Mr Benson and I could see it from the wood. I bet – '

'He's going a bit fast for a narrow road like this,' Holly interrupted as the van gathered speed. But the roar of the van's engine drowned her words.

As she tried desperately to scramble from its path, Holly's bike got tangled up with Belinda's. Frantically, Holly tried to free her handlebars.

'Leave it!' Belinda shouted, leaping off. She

grabbed Holly's arm and pulled her towards the kerb. The bikes fell with a crash.

'Look out you two,' Tracy cried. 'He's going to hit us!'

6 *The logo explained*

The girls picked themselves up off the ground, heaving great sighs of relief. All three had dived frantically to safety when the van had hurtled towards them.

Holly stood up shakily. The van had roared past and was rounding the bend at the end of the road. 'Are you OK, you two?' she asked anxiously as she helped her friends to their feet.

'That's definitely the same van I saw parked by the wood,' Belinda said, brushing herself down. 'What on earth's the matter with that man? Shooting at people, driving like a maniac. Do you think he's drunk or something?' She examined the palm of her hand for bits of gravel.

'No,' Holly, who never took anything at face value, shook her head. 'I think he saw us coming out of the Bensons' and wanted to scare us for some reason or other.' She picked up her bicycle and straightened a bent spoke.

'Maybe he just wanted to scare us . . . period!' Tracy said.

'That's two narrow escapes I've had today,' Belinda said wryly. 'This detective lark's getting a bit dangerous.'

'You can always back out if you like,' Holly said.

Belinda shook her head. 'No way.'

'Did anyone get a good look at the driver?' Tracy asked, brushing dirt off her cycling shorts.

Holly shook her head. 'I just saw that he was wearing some kind of dark jacket. I was too busy trying to avoid getting run over to get a good look.'

'Me too,' Belinda agreed. 'All I saw was this blur of white with some maniac hunched over the wheel.'

'What I did see clearly though was a yellow logo painted on the back doors of the van,' Holly declared. 'Did any of you notice it?'

Belinda and Tracy shook their heads.

'I was too busy trying to save my neck to see a darned thing,' Tracy said with a wry grin. She rubbed her leg. 'I've really bruised my knee – and I've got a tennis match tomorrow too,' she added ruefully.

'Well,' Holly said. 'Unless I'm imagining things, it was the same logo as on those envelopes. Two yellow letters entwined. An "S" and an "H".'

'Well, I reckon it stands for "stupid half-wit"!' Belinda said angrily. 'Only someone with half a brain would drive like that along a country lane.'

'Do you think it could be just a coincidence?' Tracy asked.

'That the person in the wood was driving a van belonging to the same company who sent those letters?' Belinda said. 'It doesn't sound much like coincidence to me.'

'Nor me,' Holly said grimly. 'We've got to find out what those initials stand for.'

'How?' Tracy asked.

'I could ask my mum,' Holly said. 'She might know. Or if she doesn't, she could probably tell us how to find out.'

'And the sooner we do find out,' Tracy said, 'the sooner we'll solve this mystery!'

Later that day, Holly was sitting at her desk making notes for her article from the book her father had lent her. To her surprise there was a mention of Goldenwood Lane on the very page she was reading.

Apparently the only right of access to the land behind the lane was through the paddock belonging to the owners of the end property. The whole area had once been a large estate and that had been the way into it. Anyone wanting to gain access to the land had to get the cottage owners' permission. And those owners were the Bensons!

Holly looked up from her notes and stared out

of the window. She chewed the end of her pencil thoughtfully.

There was a knock at the door. Mrs Adams came into the room, still wearing her suit.

'Had a good day, Holly?' She sat down on the bed with a sigh and took off her high-heeled shoes. She picked up one of Holly's hair clips and put it on the bedside table. 'What are you writing?'

'An article for the school magazine.'

'Anything interesting?'

Holly made a face. 'The local Rambling and Footpath Society. Dad's lent me a book.' She held it up for her mother to see.

Holly wondered if she should tell her mother about the Bensons, but she quickly decided against it. After all, until the Mystery Club had more to go on there didn't really seem to be much point. Mrs Adams could help Holly with something else, though.

'Mum . . . I don't suppose you know what the letters "S H" stand for . . . intertwined like this. I think they could be the initials of a local company.'

Holly drew the two letters on her notepad and handed them to her mother. She leaned back in her chair.

Mrs Adams frowned. 'I'm not sure, Holly. It looks familiar but . . . Any idea what kind of company?'

Holly shook her head. 'No, not really. Just that they've got a rather tatty white transit van.'

'Sorry.' Mrs Adams handed the notepad back to Holly. 'Why? Any special reason?'

'Just something Tracy and Belinda and I are looking into,' Holly said, trying not to sound disappointed.

'You could probably find out at the local library,' Mrs Adams said. 'They'll have a directory of companies. There can't be *that* many with those initials in this area.'

'Great, Mum!' Holly went to hug her mother. 'I knew you'd be able to help.'

Mrs Adams smiled, looking amused. 'I don't call that being much help.'

'Oh, it is, Mum, honestly. It really is. I'll go tomorrow morning.'

Holly was just going through the directory of local companies in the library the following day when someone spoke her name.

'Holly Adams! Fancy seeing you here! Researching that *tremendously* interesting article I asked you to do?'

Steffie Smith! Holly groaned inwardly. She might have guessed she would be here. Steffie sometimes used a word processor at the library to produce the school magazine.

'No.' Holly looked up into Steffie's pale blue

eyes. The girl's fair hair stood up on end as if she'd had a fright of some kind. 'I'm not, actually.'

'What are you doing here then?'

Holly sighed. 'If you must know, I'm looking for something.'

Steffie peered at Holly's notepad. On it, Holly had drawn the logo she had seen on the Bensons' letters and on the back of the white van.

Steffie leaned over and picked up the notepad. 'Hey, that's the logo of the Stella-Howden Company. My uncle used to work for them.'

'What?' Holly was taken aback.

'The Stella-Howden Company,' Steffie repeated matter-of-factly. 'Oh, well, I must get on.' Steffie threw Holly's pad back on the desk. 'Some of us have *important* work to do.'

Holly watched open-mouthed as Steffie disappeared behind a screen. Without knowing it, Holly's rival had given her just the information she needed!

Holly quickly thumbed through the directory. There it was: 'The Stella-Howden Company, registered office, York Road, Willow Dale.'

Excitedly, Holly copied down the address and returned the directory to its shelf. She poked her head round the screen. Steffie was entering something on to her computer.

'Er . . . Steff?'

The girl frowned and looked up. 'What?'

'That company your uncle used to work for . . . What do they do?'

'They're builders. What do you want to know for?'

Holly shrugged. 'Nothing special. Thanks, Steffie.'

Holly skipped down the stairs and out into the street. Just wait until she told the others – they'd die laughing!

'You mean she told you . . . just like that?' Tracy giggled down the telephone.

'Yup. She'd hate it if she knew she'd helped me.'

'What are you going to do now?'

'I'm going to try to find out more about them. You know, Tracy, if they're a building company I wonder if they're after the land Mr and Mrs Benson own.'

'I bet that's it. They want to buy the land. They're refusing to sell, and for some reason that company's pretty desperate to get hold of it.'

Holly frowned. 'We've got to find out why!'

'Why don't you ring Mr Welford?'

'Huh?'

'Kurt's dad. He's editor of the local paper, remember?'

'Yes, of course . . . how silly. How could he help?'

'Well, they sometimes do features on local businesses. He'll know something about them, I'm sure. I'd do it but Mom's waiting. I've promised to help her redecorate the nursery.'

'It's OK. I can do it. I'll let you know later if I have any luck.'

Excitedly, Holly searched through the Yellow Pages and found the number of the *Willow Dale Express*. She felt sure that if there was anything interesting to be discovered about the Stella-Howden Company, the local newspaper would be just the place to look!

Luckily Mr Welford was in his office when Holly telephoned.

'Why do you want to know about this company in particular?' Mr Welford asked.

Holly thought quickly. If Mr Welford knew the girls were investigating threats against the Bensons he might want to interview them himself. Holly knew Mr and Mrs Benson would hate the newspapers prying into their lives.

'Um . . . it's for a project we're doing,' she explained.

Mr Welford hesitated. 'As a matter of fact I have heard of the company, Holly. I've got a feeling we did a story on them a year or so ago. Why don't you come into the office? I'll get someone to dig out a few back numbers for you. Maybe you'll find something there.'

'That would be great. When could I come?'

'Come this afternoon if you like.'

'Thanks, Mr Welford.'

Holly put the phone down and grabbed her denim jacket from the hall cupboard.

'I'm going out, Jamie,' she called up to her brother.

Jamie came clattering down the stairs.

'Where to?'

'None of your business.'

'It's not fair,' Jamie frowned. 'Why is it you're allowed to go out wherever you like and I have to stay in on my own?'

'You're not on your own. Dad's out in his workshop. Go and keep him company.'

'He's just chucked me out,' Jamie said sulkily. 'Why can't I come with you? I'm really bored.'

Holly sighed. 'Can't you go over to your friend Philip's?'

Jamie looked sulky again. 'He's gone away for a few days. Please let me come.'

'OK, OK, but you'd better behave yourself.'

'I will. I promise.' Jamie's freckled face lit up with a smile.

At the offices of the *Willow Dale Express* the receptionist ushered Holly and Jamie into a small office.

'All the back-numbers are in the cupboard,' he said. 'They go back forty years. Was there any particular year you wanted?'

'Umm . . . I'm not sure – probably only a couple of years,' Holly said.

'Well, they're all here. Good luck!'

Jamie went to the cupboard. 'This looks dead boring,' he said, opening the door. 'What do you want to go through a load of stuffy old newspapers for anyway?'

'I just do. Look, if you're going to be a pain . . . '

Jamie held up his hands. 'No, I won't . . . I promise. How about if I go and look in the record shop?'

'Good idea,' Holly said absently, already starting to thumb through the previous year's papers.

'How long will you be?'

Holly looked up. 'What?'

'How long will you be . . . looking through these?'

'Oh . . . I don't know.'

'OK.' Jamie made a mock salute and disappeared through the door. Holly heard his footsteps running full pelt down the stairs.

It was almost three quarters of an hour before Holly found what she was looking for: a feature on the Stella-Howden Company. There was a photograph of a building site with the company logo on a big noticeboard. And standing in front of it was . . . Holly drew in her breath as she read the caption. 'Mrs Irma Stella, Managing Director of the company.' It was the woman who had called at the Bensons!

Hurrah! thought Holly. *At last we're getting somewhere!*

According to the article, the company had been formed in partnership with a Mr Richard Howden but Mrs Stella had recently bought him out.

'I plan to expand my activities,' she was quoted as saying. 'Industrial growth and speculation is what this town needs to put it on the map.'

Holly sat back, her mind racing. The company was concerned with buying up land for industrial building. That was definitely it, then! They wanted to buy the Bensons' land for development and were using threats against them to get it!

Written in the margin was a cross-reference. Holly sorted through more copies of the *Express* until she came to one with the same number.

'Local Firm Accused in Bribery Scandal,' the headline ran. And underneath, in smaller letters: 'Employee accuses local building company of bribery.'

Holly read the story eagerly. A local building firm, the Stella-Howden Company, of 29 York Street, Willow Dale, had been accused by an employee of conspiring to bribe the district council.

But to Holly's disappointment, the case had never come to court. In fact, the story gave hardly any details of the bribery accusations. Instead, the police had thrown out the employee's claim and in August of that year the employee himself had been arrested for stealing money from the company. The newspaper was unable to name him because of his impending trial.

Holly leaned forward and read the other story once more. She took out the Mystery Club notebook and made a few notes.

The next thing to do, Holly said to herself, *is pay a visit to the Stella-Howden Company. It's time to find out if our hunch is correct!*

7 *Intruder at the cottage*

Just as Holly finished making notes, Jamie appeared, licking an ice-cream cone.

'You finished?'

'Yup.' Holly closed her notebook with a satisfied bang.

'Where to now?'

'I think I'll go and visit a couple of friends.' She couldn't visit the Stella-Howden Company just yet – certainly not with Jamie in tow.

Jamie grinned cheekily. 'Not Terrible Tracy and Beastly Belinda?'

'No. They're both busy. Tracy's helping her mum redecorate the nursery and Belinda's exercising Meltdown.'

'Well, who are you going to see then?'

'An elderly couple I know in Goldenwood Lane.'

'*That* sounds even more boring than reading old newspapers.' Jamie rolled his eyes.

'Well, you don't have to come.'

'Oh, yes, I will.'

* * *

'Phew, it's a long way!' Jamie complained as he pedalled alongside Holly.

As they approached the Bensons' cottage a neighbour, walking her dog, called out.

'The Bensons have gone to the Day Centre this morning, dear.'

'Oh?'

'Great!' Jamie said scathingly. 'All this way for nothing! Why didn't you check they'd be in?'

'I didn't think,' Holly admitted. 'They can't get out much so I just assumed they'd be here. Anyway, it's not that far!'

'Far enough,' Jamie snorted.

'I suppose we'd better go back,' Holly said, disappointed. She had hoped to try to get a look at the letters from Derbyshire while she was there.

'Couldn't we explore that wood while we're here?' Jamie said. 'Seeing as we've come all this way.'

Holly shrugged. 'OK, if you like.'

As they made their way down the path beside the cottage Holly noticed a window open at the back.

'That's odd,' she said, frowning.

'What?'

'There's a window open.'

'So what?'

'They're usually pretty careful about shutting windows,' Holly said. 'Jamie, I think I'll just take a look.'

'Well, I'm not hanging around,' Jamie said, heading for the wood.

Holly looked around. The summer-house door was open but there was no sign of anyone about. She clambered up on to the coal bunker and put her ear to the open fanlight window.

When the noise of a passing plane had subsided, she heard a strange sound. Somewhere in the cottage, someone was moving furniture around. Holly frowned. Who on earth could be inside when the Bensons were out at the Day Centre?

'Mr Benson, Mrs Benson!' Holly called out, just in case they'd come back and the neighbour hadn't seen them.

There was no reply.

Determined to get inside, Holly went into the summer-house. A couple of old wire coat-hangers lay beside an old rolled-up carpet. She unbent one and climbed back on to the coal bunker. She managed to hook the wire through the small fanlight window and lift the casement catch. It came up easily. Holly pushed and the window opened.

If there is someone in there, Holly thought, *how on earth did he get in? If he'd climbed through this window, surely he would have left it open for an easy escape.*

With pounding heart, Holly clambered inside, closing the window quietly behind her.

She stood still a moment, holding her breath. Her

heart was still beating rapidly. She wished the other members of the Mystery Club were there to help.

Suddenly she was startled by a loud hammering noise. Holly realised with a shock that the sound was coming from the haunted room!

Holly opened the door as quietly as she could and crept across the narrow hallway. The heavy oak door to the haunted room was closed. With mounting trepidation Holly put her ear to the wooden panel. She could hear odd sounds from within. Someone was muttering under his breath.

Cautiously, Holly put her fingers on the brass doorknob and turned it slowly. She pushed. A cool draught struck her cheeks as the door opened.

'What the – '

A dark figure, bent over the old tin trunk that served as a fireside table, turned quickly with an exclamation of surprise. As he stood up, Holly saw he was wearing dark clothes – jeans, a baggy old combat jacket and muddy trainers. His face was covered by a balaclava helmet. Through the holes, dark eyes shone. The man was tall, with hunched shoulders.

The trunk had been forced open. A hammer lay on the floor. The man clutched a bundle of documents, the ribbon tying them together half undone.

'Who are you?' Holly said, sounding braver than she felt. 'What are you doing?'

The man quickly tried to stuff the bundle of papers into his pocket. When they wouldn't go in, he dropped them with a curse and bent to pick up the hammer.

'Get out of my way!' he snarled, his voice gruff. He brandished the hammer threateningly towards Holly.

Her mind raced. If she could just dash out and turn the key in the door, the intruder would be locked in. Then she could telephone the police quickly. She dismissed the thought. If she did that, the intruder would only escape through the window.

Before she could think of anything else the man came at her with the hammer. She dodged aside, jumping into the hallway. She slammed the door in the man's face and ran up the stairs as fast as she could, intending to yell for help from an upstairs window.

She turned to see the man had already reached the bottom of the stairs and was standing legs apart, staring up at her. For a heart-stopping moment, Holly thought he would leap up the stairs after her. His dark bright eyes seemed to glare into hers, almost hypnotising her.

Suddenly a voice called from outside.

'Holly! You in there?'

It was Jamie.

'Jamie!' Holly shouted. 'Watch out!'

As she called out to her brother, the intruder uttered a loud curse. He looked around desperately seeking a way of escape. He hurriedly unfastened the front door chain, threw open the door and ran off down the front path. Then Holly heard a shout from Jamie.

'Hey!'

Holly ran downstairs. Jamie was standing on the front path, looking dazed.

'Holly, who was that? He nearly knocked me over!'

'A burglar!' Holly exclaimed. She ran to the gate just in time to see the figure running away along the lane.

'A burglar!' Jamie exclaimed. 'Wow! How did he get in?'

'I'm not sure,' Holly said, shaking her head.

'Did he get their jewels or anything?'

'For goodness' sake, Jamie, you might ask if I'm all right.'

Jamie peered at his sister. 'You look all right to me.'

'Yes, but if you hadn't come along when you did . . . '

'Oh, great . . . so I saved you then!' Jamie grinned and ran his hand through his spiky hair. 'Wait 'til I tell my mates. A burglar . . . *wow*!'

'Come on, Jamie, let's see if anything's been taken.'

In the haunted room, the contents of the tin trunk lay scattered over the floor.

'What's this?' Jamie picked up the bundle of papers the burglar had tried to stuff into his pocket.

'Let's have a look.'

Holly finished undoing the red ribbon holding the documents together. 'Hmm . . . ' she said thoughtfully. 'These are old title deeds relating to the cottage. The proof of ownership.'

'What would a burglar want those for?'

'I don't know. Maybe he meant to take evidence of the Bensons' ownership.'

Jamie made a face. 'Sounds daft to me.' He was looking through a collection of cigarette cards. 'Hey, these are good. Look . . . old footballers!'

Holly snatched the collection from his hand. 'Don't go nosing into Mr Benson's stuff.' She put them into the trunk.

'Hey, there's someone coming along the road!' Jamie exclaimed, looking out of the window. 'It's the old couple.'

'Oh, dear,' Holly said. 'Poor Mr and Mrs Benson. I'm afraid they're in for a shock. Oh, no,' she cried. 'Something's happened to the old lady!'

Holly looked out to see Mr Benson supporting his wife as she hobbled up the garden path. They were shocked to see Holly and her brother emerge from the cottage.

'Holly!' Mrs Benson exclaimed, wincing with pain. 'What are you doing here . . . and who's this?' The old lady looked at Jamie.

'This is my brother,' Holly explained. 'He came with me to visit you. What on earth's happened?' She took the old lady's arm and helped her indoors.

'Some maniac knocked her down,' Mr Benson explained. 'The minibus that takes us to the Day Centre dropped us off down the lane and some idiot in a mask came belting round the corner and knocked her over.'

'I'm all right, Arthur,' Mrs Benson said. 'I'm not hurt. It just gave me a shock, that's all.'

'Yes, but you could have been,' Mr Benson said grimly. 'If I knew who he was I'd – '

'I've got a pretty good idea who it was,' Holly interrupted. 'The same man I found inside the cottage.'

'Inside . . . ?' Mrs Benson's hand flew to her mouth. 'But how on earth did you get inside, Holly?'

'I managed to stick a bit of wire through the fanlight and open the casement,' Holly explained. 'I'm sorry, but I could hear someone moving around and your neighbour told us you'd gone out.'

'Arthur, I thought you'd shut that window!' Mrs Benson interrupted.

Mr Benson looked glum. 'Sorry, June. The mini-bus came early. I must have forgotten.'

'But I don't know how the burglar got in,' Holly continued. 'I felt sure he would have left the big window open in case he was disturbed. And when I confronted him he had to unchain the front door. Anyway, it's OK,' Holly said, quick to reassure Mrs Benson. 'I'm pretty sure he hasn't taken anything.'

'Well, that's it,' Mrs Benson said. 'That's the last straw. We're leaving here and that's that!'

'No, June,' her husband warned. 'I told you – we're sticking by our guns. It was probably just somebody after cash or jewellery . . . a petty thief.'

'No, he came to scare us . . . I'm certain of it. And poor Holly could have been hurt,' Mrs Benson said, shaking her head.

'What I'm really annoyed about,' Holly said, 'is that we didn't manage to capture him and phone the police.'

'No!' Mr Benson blurted. 'I don't want the police involved!'

'But – '

'I said no!'

Holly sat Mrs Benson down in a chair. 'Jamie make us a cup of tea, will you?' she said to her brother.

Jamie sighed and went into the kitchen. Holly heard him opening cupboard doors, looking for things.

'Look, Mr Benson, Mrs Benson,' Holly pleaded. 'You've got to tell me what's going on. My friends and I are really worried about you. I think that intruder came here just to scare you. It looks as if someone's really got it in for you.'

Mrs Benson looked down at her hands. Then she raised her head and looked at her husband. 'Tell her, Arthur,' she said in a quiet voice.

Mr Benson sighed. 'It's all to do with that woman who called the other day.'

'Yes,' Holly said. 'I thought so.'

'She runs a firm of builders. They did some work here for the previous owners, Mr and Mrs Wynne . . . '

'Yes?'

'Well, they owned a lot of land behind the cottage and they sold it to her. Then after we bought the cottage she decided to apply for permission to build an industrial estate. But we own the rights of access. Without that, she's helpless.'

'I see,' Holly said thoughtfully. 'Why didn't she think of that before.'

Mr Benson shrugged. 'Some solicitor's mistake,' he said. 'They failed to do proper searches. Anyway, we've refused to sell her our property and now she's desperate. She's forked out thousands of pounds for the land and now she can't do anything with it.'

'And she's threatening you?'

Mr and Mrs Benson exchanged glances. 'Yes, but we're not giving in,' the old man said, shaking his head vehemently. 'She can threaten us as much as she likes.'

'What exactly is she threatening you with, Mr Benson?'

'In a word,' Mr Benson said tremulously, 'eviction.'

'Eviction!' Holly exclaimed. 'How could she do that?'

'Let's just say she's made up a lot of lies about . . . about . . . '

'About what?'

But Mr Benson would say no more.

'Don't you think you should tell your son what's going on?' Holly asked.

'He couldn't help.'

'Why not?'

'He just couldn't that's all,' Mr Benson snapped. 'And he's been involved with Irma Stella before. He knows exactly how much of a liar she can be!'

'All the more reason for – ' Holly broke off. At the mention of their son, Mrs Benson had begun to cry bitterly.

'I'm sorry, Mrs Benson.' Holly put her arm round the old woman's shoulders. 'I didn't mean to distress you.'

'That's all we're saying, young lady,' Mr Benson said firmly, patting his wife's shoulder. 'The subject is closed!'

Holly sighed. 'I'll just go and see what Jamie's doing with that tea.'

On her way to the kitchen Holly saw the pile of letters still sitting on the hall table. In the front room she could hear Mr Benson murmuring words of sympathy to his wife.

Now was her chance! Quickly, Holly found one of the letters with the Derbyshire postmark. There was no doubt about it – the writing was the same as in David Benson's book.

She opened the letter quickly. On the heading was the date, nothing more. Holly almost stamped her foot in frustration. Then turning the letter over she saw a rubber stamp on the back: 'Passed. H.M. Prison. Stonebridge, Derbyshire.'

Prison! The Bensons' son, David, was in prison!

So that's why they wouldn't talk about him. He was a criminal!

Or was he? Holly suddenly remembered the story in the newspaper about the Stella-Howden employee who had been accused of stealing money. And Mr Benson had said David had had dealings with Irma Stella before . . . She quickly replaced the letter.

* * *

'I bet he's innocent!' Holly said out loud as she and Jamie rode home. 'I bet David Benson didn't steal any money at all. I bet she framed him!'

'Who framed who?' Jamie said.

'Never you mind,' Holly said, pedalling faster. 'I've got to talk to Belinda and Tracy! Hurry up, Jamie, for goodness' sake!'

8 *Danger at midnight*

'And you reckon David's innocent?' Belinda said later, lying full length on Holly's bed. As soon as Holly had arrived home, she'd phoned her friends and asked them to come over right away.

'Yes,' Holly said confidently. 'I reckon she's just the kind of person who'd get someone put in prison for something they didn't do. The Bensons hate her, that's for sure.'

'But how on earth could she evict them? They own the cottage,' Tracy said, running her fingers through her hair.

'That's something we've got to find out,' Holly said grimly. 'And we've got to find out who that burglar was and where he came from.'

'Do you think it's the same man who took pot-shots at me and Mr Benson?' Belinda asked.

'I'm convinced of it,' Holly said. 'And it's probably the same person who was driving the Stella-Howden van.'

'Do you think he works for the company then?' Tracy asked.

'Yes. I bet that beastly Irma Stella's employed him to frighten the Bensons so they'll get fed up and sell her the cottage.'

'I think we should write to David straight away,' Belinda piped up. 'Now we know where he is, what's stopping us?'

'Nothing,' Holly said, taking a pen and paper from her desk.

'What are you going to say?' Tracy asked.

'I'll just say we're three friends of his parents and we're worried because they're being menaced by Irma Stella . . . ' Holly hesitated.

'And?' Belinda said.

Holly looked thoughtful. 'And she's not only sending someone to frighten his parents, but she's threatening them with blackmail too.'

'That sounds OK,' Tracy said.

'We'd better say that the Bensons have told us David already knows Mrs Stella,' Belinda volunteered. 'Then he'll understand why we're so worried.'

' . . . and that they refuse to go to the police,' Tracy added. 'Otherwise he'll wonder why we don't tell the police ourselves.'

'Right,' Holly agreed.

She finished writing and read through what she had put. 'That sounds perfect. Just enough to let him know what's going on.' She sat back. 'Good. Now what we've got to do is try to find out more about this blackmail business.'

'And try to prove David's innocence,' Tracy added.

'Do you think those Stella-Howden people realise we're investigating the mystery?' Belinda asked, a worried expression crossing her face. 'After all, that bloke with the gun saw me, then you thought the van driver saw us all leaving the house that day.'

Holly shook her head. 'I doubt it. They probably just think we're friends of the Bensons and that scaring us will scare them too, if you see what I mean.'

The other girls nodded.

'If you give me the letter,' Tracy said, 'I'll post it on my way home. With a bit of luck he'll get it tomorrow.'

The next morning Holly received a telephone call from Mrs Benson.

'Holly,' she said in a worried voice. 'Do you think you and your friends could come over?'

'Yes, of course, Mrs Benson. What's wrong?'

'There were more strange happenings last night – ' Mrs Benson's voice broke. 'Maybe you girls can come and investigate.'

When the Mystery Club arrived, the Bensons were visibly shaken by what had taken place at the cottage during the night.

'Look,' Mr Benson said. He showed Holly the ruined flower-beds. 'And my picket fence, completely knocked down.' The old man put his head in his hands. 'And worst of all,' he said in a muffled voice, 'someone has polluted my garden pond with insecticide. Can you smell it? All my lovely goldfish are dead!'

Holly wrinkled her nose. 'It smells like the stuff my dad sprays his rose bushes with.' She crouched down and examined the flower-beds closely. There were clear imprints of someone's trainers, the distinctive pattern of a circle on the heel. 'They're trying to frighten you.' She looked up at Mr Benson. 'To scare you into selling the cottage.'

'I know,' he said bitterly. 'And to tell you the truth they're succeeding. Come indoors, I've got something to show you . . . '

' . . . and we heard that strange noise again,' Mrs Benson was telling the other two girls as Mr Benson and Holly arrived indoors.

'What time did you hear it?' Tracy asked.

'It started about midnight . . . went on for hours.'

'Are you sure it wasn't the wind?' Belinda suggested. 'Even Meltdown was pacing around in his stable during the night. He hates the wind.'

'No, I'm sure it wasn't anything like that.' Mrs Benson's voice faltered. 'And now this . . .' She produced a letter from her cardigan pocket. 'Look!'

Holly took the envelope. There was a dirty thumbprint on the flap. Inside was a piece of paper. On it was typed:

'Will yOu sleep tOnight?'

Holly gasped and handed the letter to the other two girls.

'Oh, no!' Belinda exclaimed. 'When did this come?'

'It was on the mat first thing this morning,' Mrs Benson said shakily. 'What are we going to do? I really don't think I can stand much more of this.'

The girls exchanged glances.

Holly went to put her arm round the old lady. 'Maybe we could come and keep watch tonight,' she suggested. 'If we catch them out we'll have evidence to give the police.'

'Oh, no!' Mrs Benson said in a horrified voice. 'I can't have you girls putting yourselves in danger. What would your parents say?'

'I'm sure they'd want us to help you,' Tracy insisted.

'And I could use a break from my mother tonight,' Belinda said with a grin.

Mrs Benson managed a smile. 'Very well . . . but you'd better be careful.'

'We will, Mrs Benson,' Tracy said reassuringly. 'Don't worry about us!'

Before the girls left, Holly asked Mr Benson if she could keep the anonymous letter.

'What do you want it for?' he asked.

'I'm just keeping track of what's going on here,' Holly said. 'You never know . . . it might come in useful.'

Mr Benson shrugged. 'Keep it if you like, but I can't see what good it's going to do.'

'Did you notice the funny type on that letter?' Holly asked the others as they cycled home.

'Yes,' Tracy said. 'The "O" would only print in capitals.'

'That's why I asked Mr Benson if I could keep it,' Holly said. 'It could be significant . . . *and* it had a thumbprint on the outside. If we do find out who's vandalised the garden that print could prove useful.'

'What time shall we go to the Bensons?' Belinda asked.

'I'll ask Mum if you can both stay the night at my house,' Holly said. 'Then we'll sneak out around midnight . . . '

'Belinda, for goodness' sake, do you have to make

so much noise?' Tracy whispered as the Mystery Club crept down the stairs just after half past eleven that night.

'Sorry,' Belinda muttered. 'My Mars bar fell out of my pocket.'

Suddenly, from the upstairs landing, the sound of a door opening froze the girls into silence.

'Holly? Is that you?' In his pyjamas, Jamie tiptoed along the landing. He leaned over the banister. 'Caught you!' he exclaimed.

Holly looked up in annoyance. 'Jamie, for goodness' sake, go back to bed!'

'What are you three up to?'

'Nothing. Look, you'll wake Mum and Dad . . . '

'No chance,' Jamie grinned. 'I can hear Dad snoring like a dinosaur. If that doesn't wake Mum up, nothing will.'

'Then go back to bed and mind your own business.'

Jamie came to the top of the stairs. 'I bet you're off on some mystery. Let me come with you.'

'Heaven forbid,' Tracy muttered under her breath.

Holly went back upstairs and took hold of Jamie's arm. 'I said go back to bed!'

He shook her off. 'What will you give me not to tell Mum and Dad you're sneaking out in the middle of the night?'

'A black eye,' Belinda whispered.

Jamie made a face. 'I know,' he said, grinning

suddenly. 'You can do the washing-up for me for the rest of the week.'

'OK, OK, now go back to bed!'

Reluctantly Jamie disappeared back into his room.

'Phew!' Belinda breathed a sigh of relief. 'That was a close one.'

'He won't tell them, will he?' Tracy asked anxiously.

'I doubt it,' Holly said. 'He knows it's more than his life's worth.'

'I don't know how I'm going to keep awake,' Belinda said with a yawn. 'I stayed up late to watch that murder film on TV last night and I mucked out Meltdown's stable in the afternoon.'

Holly smiled as she closed the front door behind them. 'I expect you'll manage to. Maybe there'll be enough excitement to keep you on your toes.'

The night was warm and sultry, a threat of a thunderstorm in the air. A bank of dark clouds covered the moon as the girls took their bikes out of Holly's garage.

'I bet we get a storm,' Tracy said, looking anxiously up at the sky.

'It would be just our luck, wouldn't it?' Belinda remarked.

'It'll add to the excitement,' Holly called, pedalling on ahead. The light from her bicycle lamp threw weird shadows across the road. 'Come on, you two. 'We don't want to miss a thing!'

The girls set up their vigil under an oak tree on the edge of the wood behind the Bensons' cottage. Above their heads, the branches of the trees creaked and rustled in the wind. The moon briefly came out from behind a huge, black cloud, then disappeared. In the distance, a rumble of thunder was like a threat of doom.

Belinda sat down on her cagoule. 'I'm really not sure this is a good idea,' she complained. She ducked as Tracy threw a crisp packet at her. 'Sorry,' she said with a grin. 'It *is* a good idea. We can't let the Bensons down.' She opened the crisps and started munching.

The girls sat in silence, huddled together. An owl hooted eerily from the oak tree and, as the wind rose, the branches swayed ominously above their heads.

'Remember that movie about a gang of teen-age vampires?' Tracy whispered. 'They used to go out looking for their dinner on nights like this.'

'*Shh!*' Belinda and Holly hissed, pushing Tracy down into the grass.

'Hey,' Holly whispered suddenly. 'Look over there!'

They could see a dark figure creeping round the

edge of the Bensons' paddock. He was carrying something bulky in one hand.

'Where on earth did he come from?' Tracy whispered. 'He just appeared from nowhere.'

'I bet he's got a vehicle parked along the lane.' Holly said. 'And I bet I know exactly what type!'

Suddenly there was an enormous flash of lightning. For the first time the girls could see the figure clearly. Once again, he was wearing a balaclava helmet and a dark jacket.

'It's the same man,' Holly said excitedly.

'Wow!' Tracy exclaimed under her breath.

The figure darted swiftly across the meadow towards the Bensons' garden.

Just then there was another gigantic flash of lightning and a tremendous crack above their heads. The girls looked up. The lightning had struck a great branch of the oak tree. Sparks and flames lit up the stormy sky and a panicked flock of birds flew screeching into the night.

The girls looked on in horror as the branch began to fall . . .

With a shriek, they leapt from their hiding-place and fled in terror to the edge of the wood and into the paddock. Behind, they heard another great crack. The branch tumbled to the ground with a deafening crash.

Tracy, the fastest runner of the trio, crouched down in the long grass to wait for the others to catch up.

'Are you guys all right?' she asked, her face a picture of anxiety.

'Yes, fine,' Holly and Belinda chorused. The girls hugged one another in relief. Their vigil had almost ended in disaster.

'I expect we've made enough noise to wake the whole neighbourhood,' Holly said regretfully. 'Let alone scare that man away.'

'No!' Belinda whispered, pulling the others into a crouching position. 'He's still there, look!'

Sure enough, the figure was still lurking in the Bensons' garden. The bulky object was gone from his hand and he was crouching by the garden shed. There was a sudden bright light, quickly extinguished. For a brief moment the man's head was illuminated.

'What's he doing?' Tracy hissed above the wind.

'I don't know,' Belinda whispered. 'But it looks like something pretty dodgy.'

There was another small flash of light. 'Oh, no!' Holly cried. 'He's setting fire to the shed!'

9 *Threatening letter*

As the girls watched, the figure lurking in the Bensons' garden suddenly stood up and looked around. He cocked his head to one side, listening.

'He's heard us!' Tracy hissed.

'No, wait . . . ' Holly's voice died away. To her horror the man suddenly threw a lighted taper towards the wooden shed. There was a swift, sudden spurt of flame. The man leapt back, then turned and ran away. He vaulted the front gate and raced off down the lane.

At once, there was another sheet of flame and once more the night was lit up. Not by a flash of lightning this time. This time the Bensons' shed was ablaze!

'Quick!' Holly shouted, leaping to her feet. She dashed through the long grass of the paddock, through the orchard and towards the cottage. The others sprang after her.

'Get the hose!' Holly called. 'There's one by the back door, I saw it this morning.'

'If we can't put it out, it'll set fire to the summer-house as well!' Tracy shouted beside her.

Tracy ran to turn the tap on whilst Belinda and Holly quickly unwound the hosepipe. When the water came on, Holly aimed it at the fire. But to her horror, the water seemed only to spread the flames even further. Clearly the man had used petrol to set the fire and it would have to be smothered – but how?

The summer-house door was open. Holly ran inside and grabbed the old rolled-up carpet. She began dragging it outside.

'Quick, you two, give me a hand!'

Together the girls unrolled the carpet, lifting it high to beat out the flames.

'It's no good,' Belinda panted desperately. 'We're never going to do it!'

The heat from the fire was almost scorching her face and hair, and the smoke grew thicker.

'Yes, we will!' Holly shouted. 'Keep at it, you two.'

At last the fire was smothered. A powerful smell of smoke, petrol and burning wool filled the air. Belinda and Holly laid the smouldering carpet on the ground and stamped on it while Tracy played the hose over the last spears of flame licking around the base of the shed. Steam rose into the night air.

'Thank goodness you remembered the carpet,'

Tracy said with a great sigh of relief. She sat down heavily and passed her hand across her forehead. 'Or else we'd never have put it out. Are you guys all right?'

Holly and Belinda nodded and plonked down beside her, exhausted.

'Good job we were here,' Holly said grimly. 'Who knows what might have happened otherwise.'

'Look what I found,' Belinda said, holding up a yellow petrol can. 'It was stuffed behind the coal bunker.' She shook it. 'It's still half full. Goodness knows what he intended to do with the rest!'

'It was dead lucky he heard us, then,' Holly said. 'I bet he was going to set fire to the cottage.'

Tracy and Belinda gasped in horror. 'He wouldn't do that, surely!' Tracy said. 'Not with the Bensons inside?'

Holly shook her head. 'I don't think these people would even stop at murder to get what they wanted.'

The girls were silent. The possibility was too awful to contemplate.

Suddenly, the back door of the cottage opened and Mr and Mrs Benson appeared in their night-clothes, looking frightened.

While Tracy and Belinda explained what had happened, Holly went round to look for clues to the prowler's identity.

She shone her torch round the charred foundations of the garden shed. Frowning, she bent and picked up something from the soil. It was a badge. Once sewn on to someone's jacket, it had the remains of torn stitches around the hem. Holly put it into the pocket of her coat.

Overhead, the sky was still black as ink, although the storm had passed. *We'll have to come back in the morning,* Holly said to herself. *It's too dark to find any more clues now.*

'We can't thank you enough for what you've done,' Mrs Benson said when Holly went indoors.

'I'm sorry that carpet got scorched,' Tracy said.

'Nonsense,' said Mr Benson. 'It had been in there for years. The Wynnes left it when they moved. Some old carpet's the least of our worries.'

'You *must* tell the police now, Mrs Benson,' Tracy insisted as she took a sip from a steaming mug of hot chocolate. 'It's getting real serious. Someone's going to end up getting hurt.'

'No,' Mr Benson said. 'We'll deal with the problem ourselves. It was very good of you girls to help us, but we don't want the police involved.'

Holly looked at Tracy with raised eyebrows. She shrugged. They couldn't go to the police without Mr Benson's permission, so what on earth could they do now?

Holly excused herself to wash her hands. On

her way back from the bathroom, she stopped by the hall table. The letters were still there. If one of them contained a clue to how Irma Stella was blackmailing the Bensons, then now was her chance to find out. She hadn't dared to look last time. Finding out David's address had been risky enough.

Holly could still hear the others talking in the kitchen. Quickly she picked up an envelope with the yellow logo on the flap and took the letter out. She read it quickly.

> This is yOur last chance. If yOu dOn't sell the cOttage tO us immediately we will tell the pOlice that yOur sOn David bOught the prOperty with the mOney he stOle frOm Stella-HOwden. The hOuse will be taken away frOm yOu anyway. Things will get much wOrse if yOu dOn't agree.

So that was it! If the police believed David Benson had purchased the property with stolen funds, then the cottage would be confiscated. The Bensons would be turned out on the street!

Holly's heart thudded with excitement. She quickly folded up the letter and placed it back in the envelope.

Hearing a noise behind her, she turned. Mr Benson was standing on the threshold of the kitchen, staring at her.

'What do you think you're doing, reading my

private letters?' he bellowed angrily. 'Don't you think you owe me an explanation?'

'Oh, sorry . . . ' Tracy came into the hall. 'I knocked the letters off the table when I went upstairs to wash my hands. One must have come out of its envelope.' She smiled at Mr Benson. 'I didn't meant to leave it lying around.'

Holly shot her friend a look of gratitude.

'Are you sure you weren't reading it, Holly?' Mr Benson asked suspiciously.

'Well . . . ' Holly began, her mind searching desperately for an excuse that wouldn't be too much of a lie.

But before she could answer, Belinda came bursting into the hall.

'Hey, you two, it's almost three o'clock. We'd better be getting back.'

'Yes,' Holly looked at her watch anxiously. 'I'm sorry about the letters, Mr Benson.'

'It's all right.' Mr Benson picked up the pile and sorted out the ones with the yellow logo. 'In fact,' he went on, 'I'm fed up with them staring me in the face every time I come down the stairs . . . ' He marched into the kitchen. The girls heard the solid fuel stove door being opened, then closed with a bang.

'He's burned them!' Tracy cried.

Holly shook her head. Now their evidence was lost forever. 'I think we'd better go,' she said.

'Come on, Belinda. If Mum and Dad find out we've gone they'll be furious.'

'Keep in touch with us, Mrs Benson,' Belinda said as the elderly lady came with them to the front door. 'Let us know if you need any more help.'

Halfway down the road Tracy asked excitedly, 'What did the letter say, Holly? I'm dying to know.'

'It said they would tell the police that David bought the cottage for his parents with money stolen from the firm.'

'Oh, no!' Belinda exclaimed. 'How horrible.'

'And if they do, the cottage will be confiscated and the Bensons will be out on the street!'

'Wow!' Tracy exclaimed.

'The sooner we get more evidence against Irma Stella the better,' Holly said, a determined look on her face. 'And prove David's innocence if we can.'

'How are we going to do that?' Belinda asked.

'We could go to the Stella-Howden office, I suppose.'

'And say what?' Belinda said scathingly. '"Please can we look through your files? We're looking for evidence of blackmail and harassment." They're bound to let you.'

'If Mr Benson hadn't burned those letters . . . ' Tracy began.

'Well, he did,' said Holly. 'So now we've got to think of something else.'

'Hey,' Tracy said suddenly. 'We could make out we were doing a school project – say we were interviewing building companies about their future plans for Willow Dale.'

'That's an idea,' Holly said. 'Trouble is . . . '

'What?'

'If I go and Mrs Dracula's there, she's bound to recognise me.'

'Belinda and I could go,' Tracy said. 'We could take a clipboard and file, and make it look real authentic.'

'What do you think, Belinda?' Holly asked.

'Sounds like another crackpot scheme,' Belinda said. 'When shall we do it?'

'Tomorrow morning?'

Belinda shook her head. 'I can't. The blacksmith's coming to shoe Meltdown. Would you mind going on your own, Tracy?'

'Not at all.' Tracy's eyes shone with excitement, 'I could meet you all later to tell you how I got on.'

'OK,' Holly said. 'But be careful, Tracy. With Mrs Dracula around, you're going to need to be on your guard.'

10 *A lucky escape*

The next morning Holly went to the end of York Street with Tracy.

'I'll meet you at the ice cream parlour at . . . ' She looked at her watch. 'Midday, OK?'

'Great!' Tracy checked her clipboard. 'Do I look OK?' She had dressed in her best outfit, a spotless white button-down shirt and a short, blue skirt. She had brushed her blonde hair until it shone and wore her best blue and gold earrings.

'Yes, you look great.' Holly assured her. 'Now for goodness' sake be careful, Tracy. Remember, Irma Stella's a pretty ruthless character.'

'With luck she won't be there,' Tracy said. 'And if she is, well, I'll just be my usual sweet self! 'Bye for now!'

York Street, where the Stella-Howden office was situated, turned out to be a dingy back street near the river. On the front door of the building was a notice saying the lift was out of order. Tracy scrutinised it. The typing was odd. The letter 'O' would only print in capitals. Just like the anonymous letter that had come through the Bensons' letter-box and the threatening one Holly had sneaked a look at. Tracy tore the notice off and put it in her bag.

She opened the door cautiously. It creaked and groaned as she pushed it open and stepped inside the dim, unlit hallway of the building.

In front of Tracy was a staircase curving upwards to the first floor. The varnish was cracked and chipped. There was another notice on the lift doors saying it was not working.

Tracy wrinkled her nose. There was a strange smell about the place. Of neglect and age.

A plaque on the side of the staircase said that the Stella-Howden offices were on the third floor.

Halfway up, Tracy heard footsteps behind her on the stairs. But when she turned, there was no one there. She heard the soft click of a door closing, then there was silence.

Whoever else had been on the stairs must have gone into another office lower down. Tracy gave a sigh of relief and continued upwards.

As she stepped on to the third floor landing, a door faced her. She opened it briskly and stepped inside.

To Tracy's dismay she had obviously gone into the wrong room. Instead of an office, she was in a small, sparsely furnished kitchen. It looked neglected and dirty. But perhaps it was worth a look around.

Along one wall stood a sink unit. A kettle and an open packet of tea-bags lay on the worktop. There was a bar of yellow soap and a rusted pot scourer. Tracy could see footprints on the dusty floor. In one corner stood a wooden wardrobe. Hanging on a hook inside the door was a dark jacket. There was a light patch on the pocket where a badge had once been sewn. In the corner by the wardrobe was a black, polythene rubbish sack with some old nylon net curtain spilling out the top.

Tracy went across to the sink unit. Frowning, she crouched down to examine the footprints. They were very similar to the ones Holly had found in the muddy flower-beds at the cottage, with a distinctive circle on the heel. Whoever had vandalised the Bensons' property and set their shed on fire could well have stood in this kitchen. *Wait until I tell the others!* Tracy thought gleefully.

Just then Tracy heard footsteps ascending the stairs. She rose swiftly and went to close the door. The last thing she wanted was to be seen poking about in the kitchen. But as she pulled the door shut she heard a click as the latch dropped down.

'Oh, no!' Without success Tracy tried to release the catch. She rattled the door. *How stupid!* she thought angrily. The catch was well and truly stuck fast.

'Help!' Tracy called. She held her breath, listening. Whoever she had heard on the stairs had obviously gone. All she could hear was a telephone ringing and the distant sounds of traffic in the street. She could yell and shout for ages but it was unlikely anyone would hear. What on earth was she going to do?

Cursing her own carelessness, Tracy stood with her back against the door. She had to get out! But how? Unless she managed to break the door down, she was stuck. Even the small window on the other side of the room was tightly closed.

Tracy went across to take a closer look. The catch was covered in dust and cobwebs. It looked as if the window hadn't been opened for years.

Tracy dragged a chair over to the window. Standing on the old-fashioned radiator beneath it, she looked out over a walled courtyard. There was a wooden door in one wall. A couple of dustbins stood in a corner. Below, Tracy could see a rusted and rickety-looking fire escape leading from the window in the room next door down into the courtyard.

By the look of it, it was the only way out. But how on earth was she going to get down to the fire escape without breaking her neck?

Tracy climbed down off the chair and took a spoon and the bar of soap from the sink. She scraped all the dirt and dust off the window catch and rubbed the soap into the handle. She worked it to and fro then inserted the spoon under the catch. She heaved upwards.

To Tracy's annoyance the spoon handle bent upwards then broke off. She threw it on the floor and rubbed more soap into the hinge of the catch. After several more tries, it opened. With one strong heave Tracy pushed the window up.

She put her head outside. Just as she thought! It was ten feet or more between the window and fire escape. She couldn't imagine how people would get out if there was a real fire. Jump, she supposed.

Then Tracy remembered the sack of rubbish by the wardrobe. She shook it out. The long, nylon net curtain fell to the floor. Aside from a corner that was torn off it was all in one piece. Twisting it into a knotted rope, she tied one end to the old radiator. She threw the other end out of the window and peered out. The curtain rope stopped just short of the fire escape. *Great!* Tracy thought, clambering over the ledge.

Clutching her clipboard tightly under one arm, she carefully climbed down the rope. She almost lost her grip once, her fingers sliding a few inches down the curtain. But the knots stopped her from sliding any further. At the end of the rope, she let go and dropped down on to the fire escape.

To her horror it began to rattle and shake. A

couple of pigeons flew off a ledge, startled by her sudden appearance.

Tracy stood silently, holding her breath as she balanced precariously on the wobbly staircase. Each time she attempted to move, the staircase swayed and groaned.

Grasping the handrail, Tracy tested the first step, then the second. Eventually she reached the last three and jumped easily down on to the ground, heaving a sigh of relief. She took a deep breath to regain her balance. Then she began to make her way towards the gate in the wall. With a bit of luck, she'd be able to get out that way.

The door opened easily. Stepping through, Tracy could see she was in a back alley. At the end, the road stretched down towards the river. Tracy made her way back round to the front of the building.

'Try again,' she muttered to herself, climbing the dingy staircase once more. This time she arrived safely outside a door marked 'The Stella-Howden Company'. Drawing a deep breath, Tracy knocked.

'Come in,' a voice called.

Tracy put her head round the door. 'Hi,' she said.

The receptionist was on the telephone. She smiled at Tracy and indicated she should sit down.

Tracy sat with her legs crossed neatly, the clip-board on her lap. Looking round the office she saw a half-glazed door with 'Irma Stella' written on it. The door was slightly ajar and she could see an old metal typewriter on a desk inside.

'Yes,' the receptionist was saying. 'The dictation machine will be ready tomorrow? Great, I'll come and pick it up . . . I'll be really glad to have it back. I'm fed up with trying to read my boss's handwritten letters.'

On her desk, Tracy noticed a few sheets torn from a spiral bound shorthand pad which were covered with a heavy scrawl.

The receptionist put down the phone. 'Hi,' she said. 'What can I do for you?'

Tracy explained about the school project. 'I'm calling on local builders to find out if they have any plans to develop areas of Willow Dale,' she said. 'I really want an overall picture of how the town has changed in the past ten years and how it's going to change in the future.'

The receptionist seemed impressed. 'Well, we have been responsible for a couple of big developments,' she said. 'We had a hand in the shopping centre and in the housing estate just west of the town. Unfortunately, only a few of those new houses have sold so we've had to scale down our activities for a while.'

'Oh?' Tracy raised her eyebrows. 'What about the future?'

The receptionist hesitated. 'Well, actually, Mrs

Stella has acquired some land for an industrial park called the Goldenwood Development. But she's having a bit of trouble.'

Tracy's ears pricked up. 'What kind of trouble?'

'Well, permission's been granted but she's only got three days to buy the rights of access. Otherwise the permission will be revoked and she'll have to apply again. If you get planning permission, you have to start work within a certain period, you see.'

'It's no good building places if you can't make roads to go through them,' Tracy said with a smile.

'Right.' The receptionist stood up. 'The best thing is for you to go into the back office. You'll see lots of plans pinned to the walls there. Make some notes if you like. I'd better get on with these letters.'

'Thanks very much,' Tracy said, trying not to sound too excited.

'You could probably take a few photocopies of the old plans in the dead files cabinet,' the receptionist said. 'I'm sure Mrs Stella wouldn't mind. The photocopier's out there by the filing cabinets.'

'That's really great,' Tracy said. 'Thanks.'

In the back room, Tracy made a few hasty notes. She heard the telephone ring again and the receptionist speaking to someone.

Tracy opened the cabinet marked 'Dead Files'

and rummaged through. One marked 'Wynne' caught her eye. That was the name of the people who lived in the cottage before the Bensons!

Tracy took the file from the drawer. Inside were detailed plans of the Bensons' property. Tracy quickly made a photocopy of each of the plans and put the file back in the drawer. She took a few others out and photocopied those too, just to make her visit seem genuine. As she was replacing them she noticed a green file stuffed away at the very back of the cabinet. She was just about to take it out when she heard voices in the outer office.

'Hello, Mrs Stella. I didn't know you were coming in this morning.'

'Yes, I wanted to do a few more letters, Jane. Has that dictation machine come back yet?'

'No, I'm picking it up tomorrow.'

Tracy peeped round the door to take a look at Irma Stella. With her raven black hair, pale skin and bright red lipstick, she was just as Holly had described her.

Irma Stella was standing by the door of her office, her fingers on the handle. As she raised her hand to push her hair behind her ear, Tracy noticed a plaster on her palm.

'Make me a cup of coffee will you, Jane? Then come into my office and I'll give you those letters. I've scribbled them down but they may need changing.'

When Irma Stella had closed her door, Tracy drew a deep breath and slipped out from the back office.

'Got what you wanted?' The receptionist smiled.

'Oh, yes. Thanks!' Tracy exclaimed. 'I made a couple of photocopies. Want to see?' She desperately hoped the receptionist would say 'no'. She really didn't feel like coming face to face with Irma Stella!

The receptionist waved her hand. 'No, I'm sure it's fine.'

Tracy said goodbye and skipped out gleefully. She ran down the stairs, grinning to herself. Safely outside, she looked at her watch. It was nearly time to meet the others!

'You didn't see any plans for the Goldenwood Development?' Holly asked, taking a spoonful of her chocolate nut sundae. The Mystery Club had arranged to meet in their favourite ice cream parlour.

'No, I guess they're still with the district council,' Tracy said. 'I only looked through the 'dead files' cabinet. But the receptionist said that the permission for the development expires in three days.'

'No wonder Mrs Dracula's desperate!' Belinda exclaimed.

'But you got that notice in the same funny

type,' Holly said, writing notes in the red Mystery Club book.

'Yes, and I saw an old-fashioned typewriter on Mrs Stella's desk. I bet that's the one she uses to write those threatening letters.'

'And don't forget those footprints and the missing patch on the jacket,' Belinda suggested.

'Yeah,' Tracy said. 'Whoever's harassing the Bensons keeps their stuff in Irma Stella's office.'

'Why did you make a copy of the plans of the Bensons' cottage?' Holly asked.

'I just thought it was kind of interesting. You can see the cellar and the haunted room.'

'Well, I'm sorry I missed all the action,' Belinda said.

'Never mind,' Holly gave her friend's arm a playful squeeze. 'We've got plenty more to do before this mystery's solved!'

11 *A frightening ride*

Early the following day Belinda rode her horse along the lane towards the Bensons' house.

It was a warm morning. The sunshine just penetrated the early mist that rose from the fields and hedgerows. Belinda's tall, muscular chestnut thoroughbred went forward eagerly.

'It's been ages since we had a good gallop.' Belinda leaned forward to pat Meltdown's shining neck. The horse responded with a proud toss of his head. Belinda was an excellent rider and seemed to lose all of her awkwardness when in the saddle.

She guided Meltdown along beside the cottage and into the wood. Meltdown danced on his toes. He snorted air through his flaring nostrils and shook his head impatiently.

'Now calm down,' Belinda said soothingly. 'We're not there yet.' Shc lifted one leg and reached for the strap to lengthen her stirrups. If they were going to have a gallop along the bridle path, she would be more secure in the saddle with longer stirrups.

Once through the gate, Belinda shortened her reins and urged Meltdown into a fast trot. The thoroughbred was already warmed up by his journey from Belinda's house.

'OK, Meltdown . . . ' Belinda said. 'Here we go!'

She sat deep into the saddle and kicked her horse into a controlled canter.

'Just to let you know you've got to do as you're told,' she said, grinning as she felt Meltdown's muscles tense, ready for flight.

At last she let him have his head and he broke into a gallop. Horse and rider flew along the path, Belinda leaning forward, her heels well down, urging Meltdown on even faster. Eventually, as she came to the woodland clearing she brought him expertly back into a canter, then a trot, then eventually a walk. She leaned forward to pat his steaming neck.

'That was great, boy,' she said, her face red beneath her skullcap. 'Really great!'

Belinda stood up in the stirrups, momentarily stretching her legs. As she did so, she noticed the white van parked along the lane in exactly the same place it had been before.

I wonder what he's *doing here,* Belinda said to herself. *Snooping around, I bet. Looking for ways to cause more trouble!*

Belinda dismounted. She took off her skullcap

and hung the strap over a low branch. She slipped Meltdown's reins over his head and took a piece of twine from her pocket. She fixed it to the reins, then tied them to a tree trunk. She patted the thoroughbred's neck.

'You stay here and have some grass, Meltdown. I'm just going to take a closer look at that van. I won't be long.'

She crashed her way through the undergrowth, climbed the fence and ran across the field to the van. Painted on the back was the now familiar Stella-Howden logo. Furtively, Belinda looked through the window. She tried the handle of the back door. It opened.

'Wow!' Belinda breathed. 'What a bit of luck!'

Making sure no one was around, she climbed inside and shut the door gently behind her.

Lying on the floor was a shotgun. Beside it was a box containing cartridges. They looked like the same type she had found in the wood after the stranger had shot at her and Mr Benson. She put two in the pocket of her jodhpurs and took another look around. Stacked in another corner of the van was a plastic container with a skull and crossbones sticker on the side. She took a quick sniff. It smelled just like the insecticide used to poison the Bensons' fish pond.

Belinda grinned gleefully. This was just the kind of evidence they needed. All they wanted now was the man's identity and they would be home and dry!

She was just about to clamber out of the van when she heard footsteps. The driver's door opened, then slammed shut. To her horror, someone turned on the ignition and the engine roared into life. Before she could do anything to prevent it, the van roared off down the road with Belinda crouched helplessly inside!

Belinda kept well down. She knew if the van driver glanced in his mirror he might well be able to see her. Then what would she do?

After about ten minutes' fast drive the van screeched to a halt. Belinda heard the door slam and footsteps walking away.

When everything was quiet, she got to her knees and looked out of the back window. The van was parked outside a large house in a tree-lined avenue.

Where on earth was she? Belinda did not recognise her surroundings at all. There was no sign of the van driver, but in an upstairs window of the house Belinda could see movement. Someone was standing by the window.

Belinda screwed her eyes up against the light. It was a woman peering into a hand mirror, applying lipstick. Then she brushed out her long, black hair. Although she had never actually seen Irma Stella, Belinda guessed it was she.

When Belinda decided the coast was clear, she quietly opened the back of the van and jumped out. She closed the door behind her. Then, looking over her shoulder, she crept round the back of the van. She wanted to get a closer look at the house.

Just then Belinda heard a shout. To her horror, the tall woman was hurrying down the garden path towards her. She was wearing a tracksuit and trainers.

'Hey!' the woman shouted.

There was nothing to do but run!

At the end of the road, a pair of wrought-iron gates led to a public park. If Belinda could reach them quickly, she could soon hide amongst the trees. She glanced over her shoulder. The woman was still hurrying after her. Belinda wiped her brow, wishing Meltdown was there so she could just leap on his back and escape.

In the park, there was a children's play area full of youngsters. Belinda ran inside and crouched down behind the climbing frame. She was hoping that in her navy blue jodhpurs and an old green sweatshirt she would blend in with the colours of the play area.

Several children stared at her curiously. Belinda grinned and held her finger to her lips. Looking over the top, Belinda saw the woman standing on the pathway looking confused. Then, to Belinda's immense relief, the woman spun on the heel of her trainers and walked back through the park gates.

'Phew!' Belinda took off her glasses and wiped the steam off the lenses on to her jodhpurs. She took out a handkerchief and wiped her brow. Thank goodness the woman hadn't been a good runner. She would have caught up with Belinda in no time!

Now, Belinda said to herself, trying to keep a cool head, *how on earth can I get back to collect Meltdown*?

Holly had been preparing lunch when the phone rang for the second time that morning.

The first caller had been Mr Benson, who'd told Holly that his wife had seen someone lurking about. 'But he ran off when she went outside to hang up some washing,' he'd said in a worried voice.

The next caller was Belinda. She sounded frantic.

'Holly!' she said urgently. 'Could you whiz over to Goldenwood Lane and pick up Meltdown from the wood?'

'Where on earth are you then?' Holly asked in surprise. 'I thought *you* were riding in Goldenwood this morning. Mr Benson's just called to say that man's been hanging around again.'

'Yes, he was over there in his van.'

'Well, where are you then?'

'I'm in Parkmead.'

'Parkmead!'

Holly knew the residential area was on the north side of the town. She scratched her head. 'How on earth did you get over there?'

'I'll tell you later. My money's running out. Listen, I've left Meltdown tied to a tree. Can you get him and ride him home for me?'

'Ride him home? Oh, Belinda, I don't know if I can.'

'Don't be daft, Holly, of course you can. You've ridden him before.'

'Yeah, and the last time I fell off!'

'Everyone falls off some time or other,' Belinda said. 'You'll be fine. I wouldn't ask you if I didn't think you could do it.'

'Well . . . if you're sure.'

'Of course I'm sure. Just be firm with him. He's a poppet once you get to know him.'

'OK. But, Belinda, what on earth's happened?'

'I can't tell you now. I only had twenty pence and it's almost run out. It won't take me long to walk home. I'll tell you everything later.'

There was a click and the line went dead.

Holly found Meltdown still grazing contentedly in the woodland clearing. He raised his head and whinnied in greeting as she approached. She held out her hand and let him explore her fingers with his nostrils.

'Good boy.' Holly patted the horse's huge, muscled neck. She lifted the saddle flap and tightened his girth then untied the rope and pulled his reins over his head. She took Belinda's skullcap from the tree and buckled it tightly under her chin.

Feeling slightly nervous, she gathered the reins into one hand and put her foot into the stirrup.

'Steady, boy,' she said, trying to sound in control.

Holly mounted the thoroughbred with ease. She patted his neck again.

'Look, Meltdown,' she said, 'I'm the boss, OK? Belinda says you're a poppet so you'd better prove it to me, OK?'

Holly gathered the reins together and pressed her heels gently into the thoroughbred's shining flanks. Meltdown walked obediently along the path.

Gaining confidence, Holly managed to urge Meltdown into a trot. Refreshed by his rest, the horse danced along. For a brief moment, Holly thought she might have difficulty controlling him. Remembering Belinda's instructions when she had ridden him before, Holly shortened her reins to hold him in check.

'Whoa, old boy,' she said. 'Don't be too eager.'

But Meltdown was in an energetic mood and Holly could see he was only wearing a snaffle. An inexperienced rider needed a much harsher bit to control him properly. Holly gripped the saddle tightly with her knees. If Meltdown did decide to buck then she had no choice but to make sure she was ready for it.

Suddenly, without warning, a figure popped up from the undergrowth. It was the man with the binoculars.

'Oh!' he said in a startled voice. 'Sorry, I . . . '

But Holly heard no more. Meltdown had shied violently sideways as the figure appeared.

'Meltdown!' Holly shouted. 'Whoa, boy! *Whoa!*'

But the thoroughbred ignored her. Spooked into panic, he bolted down the bridle path as fast as his legs would carry him. Holly ducked to avoid low branches as the horse plunged off the path and through the undergrowth. He leapt over a fallen tree with Holly hanging on grimly to the reins. She grabbed a handful of his chestnut mane and held on tightly.

Together, horse and rider headed along the bridle path. Meltdown swerved as he galloped along the edge of the paddock and down beside the Bensons' cottage. Holly leaned forward in the saddle. She knew it was no use fighting the frightened creature. She had to let him have his head!

Suddenly, Holly realised they were heading towards the main road. She could hear the roar of traffic as Meltdown sped towards the junction. If Meltdown careered on to the highway, there could be a terrible accident. She had to stop him now – before it was too late!

Thrusting her heels well down in the stirrups, Holly sat back in the saddle and pulled on the reins with all her might.

'Whoa, Meltdown!' she shouted as the sound of the traffic grew nearer and nearer. *'Whoa!'*

The horse ignored her. Fighting to escape Holly's iron grip on the reins, he put his head down, straining at the bit.

Holly gasped. If she didn't watch out she would topple right over the top!

Pulling with all her might, she managed to get Meltdown's head up.

'Whoa, boy!' she cried again. 'Whoa!' Holly leaned back and pulled again.

To her tremendous relief she felt the thoroughbred begin to respond. Beneath her aching legs the horse's strong muscles tightened as he began to dig in his hooves in response to her commands. He slowed, then, skidded to a halt.

Taken by surprise, Holly nearly flew over his head. With a strength she did not know she possessed, she grabbed a fistful of his mane and managed to hang on.

The thoroughbred stood still at last, trembling and sweating beneath Holly's firm hands.

'Good boy,' she murmured, patting his sweating neck. 'There's a good boy.'

In front of her, hardly more than a metre from her path, a huge lorry thundered past. Her legs shaking, Holly leaned forward and patted Meltdown's neck.

'A poppet, eh?' she said ruefully, pushing her hair back from her perspiring face. 'More like a racehorse if you ask me!'

Meltdown behaved perfectly for the rest of the way home. Subdued by his panic-stricken flight, he trotted obediently back to Belinda's house in the prosperous area of Willow Dale.

Belinda was waiting anxiously for Holly's return. Tracy arrived at the same time, summoned by an anxious telephone call from Belinda.

'I knew you'd be OK,' Belinda said, unsaddling Meltdown and rubbing him down. 'Did he behave himself?'

'He was fine until that man with binoculars scared him half to death,' Holly explained.

'Oh, no!' Belinda exclaimed. 'He's not hurt, is he?' She bent down to examine the thoroughbred's legs.

Holly laughed. 'He's fine. And so am I. Thanks for asking.'

Belinda looked up and grinned. 'I can *see* you're all right. In fact you look as if you quite enjoyed it.'

'Well . . . ' Holly raised her eyebrows. 'Actually it was great – apart from almost colliding with that lorry.'

'Poor old Meltdown.' Belinda stood up and rubbed her face into her horse's mane.

'For goodness' sake,' Tracy said impatiently. 'Tell us what happened to *you*, Belinda, I'm dying to know.'

'Me too,' Holly said.

Belinda related her adventure. 'The worst thing was,' she said, 'waiting until the driver had gone into the house before I dared get out. I was petrified he'd come round to the back of the van and find me hiding in it.'

'Wow!' Tracy exclaimed, wide-eyed.

'I didn't recognise the area at first. But when I ran away I saw a sign that said "Parkmead". Luckily there was a phone box just along from the park gates so I could call you and tell you about Meltdown.'

'Did you got a good look at the driver?'

Belinda shook her head. 'No. I only saw the top of the back of his head. Mind you, at least we know one thing now.'

'What?' Holly and Tracy chorused.

'That the van driver and the man with binoculars are two different people.'

'That's right,' Tracy said thoughtfully. 'But they could still be working for Irma Stella. She could have a whole army of people doing her dirty work!'

'I'd better ring Mr Benson,' Holly said. 'He

phoned me earlier to say they'd seen someone lurking around. Now we know who it was!'

'You can tell him he's gone,' Belinda said. 'Use the extension in my room.' Belinda hung Meltdown's saddle on its rack. 'Mum's out so she won't be there to ask what you're up to.'

Holly went through the luxurious kitchen of the chalet-style house and up the staircase to Belinda's bedroom.

As usual, Belinda had left her television on, and the room was an absolute mess. Holly honestly didn't know how Belinda managed to find a thing. In fact it took Holly a couple of minutes to locate the telephone, buried under a pile of clothes and a stack of riding magazines. She sat down and dialled the Bensons' number.

When there was no reply Holly put the phone down with a sigh.

Back in the stable yard, Belinda was hosing down Meltdown's hind legs.

'Any luck?' Tracy sat on the post and rail fence, watching the proceedings.

Holly shook her head. 'Nope. I'll try again later. I can't think where they might have gone. Maybe we should go over there again.'

'I can't. I've promised to play table-tennis with Kurt tonight,' Tracy said.

'Neither can I,' Belinda piped up. 'Mother Dear's got some friends coming over to play bridge.

I promised her I'd stay in and help with the food.'

'Help eat it, you mean,' Holly said with a grin.

'Can you go?' Tracy asked Holly.

Holly shook her head. 'No, I've got to Jamie-sit. Mum and Dad are going to the pictures. I'll try to phone the Bensons again. After all, time's running out for Mrs Stella. It may be running out for the Bensons too!'

12 *Underground discovery*

On Saturday morning the Mystery Club hurried over to Goldenwood Lane. Holly had tried to phone Mr and Mrs Benson several times the previous evening, only to learn from the operator that their phone was out of order.

'They're hoping to get someone out to mend it later today,' Holly told the others.

They soon arrived at the cottage, but there was no reply to their knock.

'Mrs Benson!' Holly called anxiously through the letter-box. Two empty milk bottles stood by the step, one with a note tucked inside. 'Mrs Benson, it's Holly!' she called again.

'I can't hear anyone,' Belinda said, her ear to the door.

'Maybe they're still in bed,' Tracy suggested. She looked at her watch. 'It's still pretty early.'

They stood by the front door, wondering what to do. The milkman drew up in his float. He came down the path, whistling.

'Hi,' Holly said. 'We can't seem to make anyone hear. I guess we're too early for them.'

'They're usually up by the time I come,' the milkman said with a frown. 'I hope they're OK.' He took the note from the empty milk bottle. 'Ah,' he said, 'one extra pint. The newspaper's gone from the letter-box so I should think they're up. I'd knock a bit harder if I were you.' He put three fresh bottles of milk on the step and went off, still whistling.

'I'll just go round the back and see if they're out in the garden,' Belinda said. 'If not, we'll have to come back a bit later.'

Walking round by the side of the house, Belinda stopped suddenly. She could definitely hear voices inside now. Maybe they had the radio on and hadn't heard their knock?

The door to the summer-house was open. Perhaps Mr Benson was in there. Belinda decided to go and see.

But the summer-house was empty. Belinda sighed. She turned to leave, but suddenly remembered something odd. The old carpet they had used to smother the flames of the burning shed the other night had been rolled up against one side of the summer-house. She hadn't thought anything of it at the time but the first time she had seen the summer-house, the carpet had been laid down on the floor. And after the fire, Mrs Benson said it didn't matter that it was scorched. It had been in the summer-house for years, long before they bought the cottage.

Curious, Belinda pushed the door open further and went inside. There was a musty smell of old wood and decay. A pile of old boxes held a few mouldy apples and a couple of broken deckchairs were stacked in one corner. Frowning, Belinda bent down on one knee.

What on earth? she asked herself suddenly. In the grimy wooden floor, previously covered by the old carpet, was what looked like a trap-door. Heart thudding with excitement, she ran back to the others.

'Hey, come and look what I've found!'

In the summer-house, the girls stood looking at the trap-door.

'I wonder where it goes to?' Tracy said, crouching down. She tried to insert her fingers between the edge of the door and the floorboards, but there was only a small gap. 'We need something to prise it open.'

'By the way,' Belinda said suddenly, 'I'm sure I heard voices in the cottage. It's either the radio or someone's inside and they're not answering.'

Holly stood up and looked around. Spying an old pair of hedge clippers under one of the boxes, she wedged the points under the ridge in the floor and prised upwards.

'This should do it,' she said with a grunt. Slowly, the door began to move. 'Quick . . . put your fingers under it.'

Together the girls heaved. The hinge creaked and groaned as they pulled. The door opened suddenly, and the girls sat down with a bump.

'I knew that would happen,' Tracy said with a laugh. She stood up and brushed the dirt off her jeans, coughing at the cloud of dust that rose up as the trap-door hit the floor.

Holly looked outside but no one had come out of the house to see what the noise was about.

Belinda was peering into the hole. A smell of dampness and stale air filled her nostrils.

'I can't see a thing,' she said, frowning into the gloom. 'Anyone got a torch?'

'I bet there's one in the shed.' Tracy ran outside. She came back quickly. 'I couldn't find a torch,' she said breathlessly, 'but there were some matches. Want to go first, Holly?'

'Er . . . OK,' Holly replied, hesitation in her voice. She struck a match.

The brief flare of light showed a steep brick staircase leading down.

To Holly's annoyance, a cold draft blew out the flame. She turned to the others. 'There's a stairway down. We'll have to feel our way.'

Warily the girls descended the steep flight of

steps into the darkness. Tracy clutched Holly's sweatshirt for guidance. Behind her, Belinda almost lost her footing and tumbled into them.

'Careful!' Holly cried.

'Sorry,' Belinda muttered. 'Light another match, Holly. It's like the black hole of Calcutta in here.'

Suddenly Holly's feet hit a hard, paved floor. She struck another match and looked round quickly before the draft blew it out. She shivered in the pitch darkness.

Behind her Tracy gasped. 'What kind of place is this?'

'A place where vampires go during the daytime,' Belinda whispered eerily. She tweaked Tracy's hair at the back.

'Oh, Belinda!' Tracy said with an uncertain laugh. 'For goodness' sake!'

They were in a low-roofed room, the white-washed brick walls black in places with mould and decay. Holly shuddered again as a sudden chill crept over her. She hurriedly struck another light. A spider scuttled away, scared by the sudden flame. The girls just had time to see a wooden wine rack all along one wall, and a pile of what looked like coal against another.

'It's the cellar!' Belinda said. 'Don't you remember Mr Benson telling us there was one? It was on that old plan you copied, Tracy.'

Tracy took the box of matches, struck one and

walked round. 'That's right,' she said. 'It's really creepy isn't it?'

'I wonder where it goes,' Belinda said. 'Come over here, Tracy, I think there are some more stairs.'

'Shh,' Holy said suddenly. 'I can hear voices.'

Sure enough, from above their heads came the sound of muffled voices.

'That's Mr Benson,' Holly murmured.

'And Mrs Benson. Who are they talking to?' Tracy said in a hushed voice.

Holly shook her head. 'I don't know. It sounds as if they're having an argument. You don't think it's Mrs Dracula, do you?'

The girls stood, holding their breaths, silently listening to the voices above. The sudden scrape of a chair on a flagstone floor indicated they were below the kitchen.

'Let's have a look at those other stairs,' Holly suggested.

Belinda led the way to the staircase at the other end of the cellar. In the brief, bright flame of Holly's match they could see the outline of another trap-door in the ceiling.

'Hey, what's that?' Tracy crawled up the stairs and pulled something from the edge of the trap-door. She climbed back down.

Holly lit another match. 'It's a piece of material,' she said, puzzled. 'A net of some kind . . . '

'Just like those scraps that had been spilled from

Mrs Benson's sewing box in the haunted room!' Belinda said.

'Of course,' Holly said. 'This part of the cellar must be below the haunted room.'

Holly climbed upwards and put her shoulder against the door. She heaved, but it moved only a tiny bit.

'Come and give me a hand, you two.'

Mounting the steps beside her, Tracy put her shoulder to the door. Together, the girls heaved upwards. The trap-door rose a little way then rebounded. With a cry Tracy lost her footing and tumbled down the steps.

'You OK?' Belinda helped her to her feet.

'Sure,' In the darkness, Tracy brushed herself down.

'Hey, you two,' Holly whispered. 'I can see something.'

This time she had managed to push the door a little way open by herself. Through a crack of light Holly could see the maroon fringed edge of something.

'It's the edge of a rug, or something. Yes, it is. We're definitely underneath the haunted room.'

'I bet this is how Rebecca Smythe's lover got in,' Tracy said. 'They used to meet in secret, remember?'

'I expect when the old house was still here,' Belinda added, 'they used to bring wine up direct from the cellar to the dining hall. Those doors in the summer-house were probably once outside the original walls.'

'Yes,' Tracy said. 'And I bet this is how that intruder got in too.'

Holly came down the steps. 'You're right, Tracy. But how did he know it was here? No one else seems to. The door has always been covered by that old rug.'

Belinda shrugged. 'I've no idea,' she said.

'I know!' Tracy said suddenly. 'Remember, Stella-Howden did some renovation work on this house. The doors must be on that old plan I copied!'

'And that's why the rug was all messed up,' Holly said. 'Mrs Benson said she thought it had been nailed down. Well, she was right – it had! But what she didn't realise was that the so-called "ghost" had come up underneath and pushed it away.

'And, speaking of ghosts . . . ' By the light of a match she held up the scrap of shimmery white material. 'I bet if we compared it, this would match that old net curtain Tracy found at the Stella-Howden office!'

'This is brilliant.' Belinda punched the air with excitement. 'Really brilliant. Let's go and tell the Bensons!'

Out again in the daylight, the sun dazzled their eyes.

'We know they're in,' Holly said. 'Let's *make* them hear this time!'

As she spoke, they heard the front door slam and the sound of footsteps hurrying down the path. Then car doors slammed and the engine gunned into life. The driver revved the engine loudly then roared off down the road. Holly quickly latched the summer-house door and followed the others round to the front.

'Mr Benson's gone off in a green car with someone,' Belinda said, looking puzzled. 'They seemed in a mighty rush if you ask me.'

Holly frowned. 'How odd. I saw a green car when we arrived. It was parked a bit further down the road.'

'Who on earth do you think it is?' Belinda asked.

'Whoever it was,' Tracy said, 'they were in a terrible hurry to get Mr Benson away from the house.'

'You don't think . . . ?' Belinda began. The girls looked at one another, horror dawning on their faces.

'What?' Holly said.

'You don't think Mrs Dracula's sent someone to kidnap him?'

'Don't be daft . . . ' Belinda began unconvincingly.

'Quick,' Holly said. 'Let's go and see if Mrs Benson's all right!'

They ran to bang on the front door. To their surprise it opened immediately.

Mrs Benson looked flustered. 'Girls! Where did you come from?'

'We – we were round the back,' Holly said breathlessly. 'We saw your husband being taken away. What on earth's happened?'

Mrs Benson laughed. 'Taken away! Don't be silly, dear. He just gone out with . . . with a friend.' She picked up the milk bottles. 'Are you coming in? You three look in a bit of a state. What *have* you been up to?'

Holly sighed. 'We'd better come in and tell you.' She looked down the lane after the speeding car. In spite of Mrs Benson's reassurance, Holly still wasn't convinced the old man hadn't been driven off against his will.

'I tried to telephone you last night,' Holly began, 'but the phone's out of order.'

Mrs Benson nodded. 'Yes, they're supposed to be coming to repair it today.'

Mrs Benson listened in amazement as Holly told her what they'd found in the summer-house.

'Well, well,' she said. 'I had no idea. We've never taken that rug up.'

'And you'd never seen those old plans?'

Mrs Benson shook her head. 'David dealt with everything for us.'

'But you've got the title deeds. That man was trying to pinch them, we thought.'

'Yes, the very old ones. David was going to try to

trace the history of the place but I've never looked at them. Of course, all that was before . . . ' She hesitated. 'Before that awful woman told all those lies about him.'

Tracy saw Mrs Benson glance at the clock on the wall. A worried frown passed across her face.

She leaned forward. 'Mrs Benson, are you *sure* Mr Benson's OK?'

Mrs Benson drew a deep breath. 'Actually, I *am* worried about him. He's gone . . . '

'Where?' the girls chorused.

'He's gone to that woman's office,' Mrs Benson blurted. 'Oh, dear . . . I shouldn't really have told you.'

'Mrs Stella!' Holly exclaimed. 'What on earth for?'

'He's fed up with everything. He's got a friend to take him to confront her . . . to say he's going to the police if she doesn't stop harassing us and telling lies.'

Mrs Benson took out her handkerchief and blew her nose. 'I tried to stop them. I said it wouldn't do any good,' she went on tearfully. 'Nobody believed us before and they won't now. I'm afraid Arthur's just at the end of his tether.'

All of a sudden there was a lot of noise out in the lane. Everyone rushed to the window.

'What on earth?' Holly exclaimed.

Outside the cottage a huge yellow JCB digger was

pulling up by the gate. As the girls watched, the driver began to rev the engine loudly. A cloud of black smoke came from the exhaust. The noise was like thunder echoing along the quiet lane.

The driver cut the engine while he read through a piece of paper on the dashboard. Then he started to rev up the engine once more. He backed the huge machine into the lane. With a scrape of gears, the digger began to edge menacingly towards the cottage.

Holly stood with her hand over her mouth in horror. Her grey eyes were wide with disbelief.

'What's going on?' Tracy cried. 'What's that guy going to do?'

Holly shook her head, unable to believe what was happening. 'I think perhaps . . . '

'He *is*,' Belinda shouted. 'He's going to knock down the fence and plough up the front garden!'

'Oh, no!' Tracy cried. 'We've got to stop him!'

13 *Race against time*

The three girls rushed forward, waving their arms.

'Hey . . . stop!'

The driver ignored their cries. At the cottage door, Mrs Benson held her clenched fist to her mouth. She stared as if mesmerised at the great machine. Suddenly she gave a small cry. Her knees gave way and she sank to the ground.

The girls ran back to her. Tracy put her arms under the old lady's shoulders and held her up, leaning her back against the door frame.

'Are you all right, Mrs Benson?'

Mrs Benson took several deep breaths. She struggled to her feet.

'Yes, I'm all right. What's that man doing, Tracy?'

'I'm not sure. You go inside while we find out, OK?'

'No – I'm staying here.'

To everyone's horror, the digger edged nearer to the fence.

'He can't *really* mean to knock the fence down,

can he?' Holly said incredulously. 'He must be crazy.'

'If he comes from Irma Stella and her rotten company I bet you anything that's exactly what he's going to do,' Belinda said grimly.

Holly ran forward again, waving her arms. This time, the operator saw her. To her relief, he cut the engine and climbed down from the cab.

'What's up?' he asked. 'Do you want to get knocked down or something?'

'What on earth are you doing?' Holly gasped.

'What's it look like?' The man tipped his yellow safety helmet to the back of his head.

'It looks like you're going to ruin the garden,' Tracy piped up, joining her friends beside the huge machine.

'Right first time. You'd better get out of the way before you get hurt.' He made to turn round and climb back into the cab. Holly clutched his arm.

'You can't!' she cried. 'Who told you to do this?'

The man shrugged. 'Got my orders,' he said.

'Who from?' Holly asked.

The man produced a piece of paper from the pocket of his overalls. 'The local council,' he said.

'Let me look.' Holly snatched the paper from the man's hand. 'Hey,' she said to the others, 'look at this.'

The paper was apparently a permit to go ahead with a road widening scheme.

'Why on earth didn't anyone tell the Bensons about this?' Belinda exclaimed.

'Because it's a fake,' Holly snorted. 'Don't you see? It's done on that same wonky typewriter as that other stuff from Stella-Howden.' She pointed to where the 'O' was printed only in capitals.

Belinda peered closer, adjusting her spectacles. 'Wow! So it is!'

'This is definitely a fake,' Holly said, handing the paper back to the digger driver.

'Oh, yeah,' he remarked. 'Who says?'

'I do. Look, for goodness' sake – the council wouldn't just start a road widening scheme without telling the occupants! It's ridiculous.'

The man shrugged. 'It's not up to me to ask questions. I just do as I'm told. Anyway, why should I take any notice of a kid like you?'

'Kid!' Belinda blustered.

'Look,' Holly said urgently. 'I can prove it – if you'd just wait a bit.'

The driver was putting the paper into his pocket. 'Sorry.' He climbed up into the cab and switched on the engine. He moved a lever forward and revved up. 'It's more than my job's worth to take any notice of some kids,' he shouted. 'Far as I'm concerned, this fence and the trees are coming down.'

'Holly, we've got to stop him!' Belinda cried desperately.

'Come on!' Tracy grabbed her arm. 'Let's stand in front. He can hardly run us over, can he?'

'Want to bet?' Belinda said doubtfully.

'Well, there's only one way to find out!'

Pulling Belinda along with them, Holly and Tracy ran to stand by the fence. They stood side by side, arms outstretched, in the path of the huge machine.

The driver leaned from the cab. 'Out of the way, you three!' He moved another lever and began to edge slowly forward.

'Oh, no!' Belinda gulped. 'He's going to run us down.'

Holly shook her head. 'He won't . . . he can't!'

Tracy put her hand over her eyes. By now the machine was so close they could see the rust spots on its bonnet. Holly squeezed her eyes shut. She felt Belinda clutch her hand as the heat from the engine seared her face.

Suddenly the engine cut out and there was silence. Holly opened her eyes to see the driver climbing down from the cab. He came towards them menacingly.

'Look, you lot!' He tried to grab Tracy's arm but she dodged away. 'What are you? Blooming conservationists or something?'

'Please . . . ' Holly said. 'Please believe us. Those instructions you've got are fake. Would we stand here risking our lives if it wasn't true?'

By now, a few of the Bensons' neighbours had come out to see what all the noise was about.

At her words, they cheered.

'These girls are right, man,' one of them called out. 'You can't just ride rough-shod over these people's property. Where did your instructions come from?'

The driver shrugged. 'The council. My boss just said he'd had the order and I was to carry it out.'

'Look,' Holly said, 'will you just give us time to prove what we say is true?'

The driver looked at his watch and shook his head. 'I dunno,' he said. 'I've got another job to go to. I don't get paid for standing around chatting, you know.'

'Can't you go there first?'

He shook his head. 'No, sorry. My orders are to do this one first.'

'Please,' Tracy pleaded. 'Give us half an hour.'

The driver took off his hard-hat and scratched his head. He sighed. 'OK, then. I'll have my tea and read the paper. Half an hour, mind you, and then . . . ' He waved his hand at the cottage. 'I'm carrying out my orders and that's that. If the council says the road's got to be widened, then it's got to be widened.' He shrugged. 'Sorry.'

He climbed up and took a lunchbox and flask from the cab.

'Thanks.' Holly breathed a sigh of relief. 'Come on, you two. We've got to be quick!'

Mrs Benson stood by the gate, still looking pale and shaken.

'What did he say?' she asked.

'He says there's a road widening scheme at this end of the lane and they're taking your front garden.'

Mrs Benson's hand flew to her mouth.

'But don't worry,' Holly added quickly. 'We're positive it's one of Irma Stella's tricks. We're going to try to get proof.'

'But?'

'We'll explain later. Now don't worry, I'm sure we'll get it sorted out. Come on, you two!'

The girls grabbed their bikes, but Holly suddenly realised Tracy wasn't with them.

'Come *on*, Tracy!' she shouted.

Tracy caught up as they pedalled frantically along the lane. They had half an hour to get to York Street, somehow find proof the document came from Irma Stella and get back to Goldenwood Lane. It seemed impossible!

'We'll never do it!' panted Belinda. As she spoke, her bike suddenly slewed sideways on gravel and she went sprawling.

The others skidded to a halt.

'Belinda!' Holly leapt off her bike and went to help her friend. 'Are you OK?'

Belinda sat in the road, rubbing her elbow. 'Great!' She scrambled to her feet. She climbed back on and put her feet on the pedals. 'Oh, no!' she cried, looking down. 'I've got a puncture!'

Tracy glanced at her watch. 'What are we going to do now?'

'You go on,' Belinda gasped. 'I'll go back and keep Mrs Benson company. Go on.' She gave Holly a push. 'Hurry!'

Holly and Tracy exchanged glances. Reluctantly, Holly nodded and they sped away.

'If we're late,' Holly shouted to Belinda over her shoulder, 'do what you can to stop him!'

Belinda watched as the girls sped out of sight. She turned with a sigh and began to make her way back to the cottage.

Holly and Tracy pedalled furiously along the lane. Hardly stopping at the junction with the main road, they hurtled towards the railway crossing.

To the girls' dismay, just as they approached the gates, the lights began to flash and the sound of the siren warned of an approaching train.

'Maybe we can beat it!' Tracy gasped.

'Don't be daft.' Holly screeched to a halt, Tracy beside her. 'Killing ourselves won't do any good.'

The girls waited impatiently for the train to pass. Tracy glanced at her watch.

'We've been ages already,' she said, shaking

her head. 'Belinda was right; we're never going to do it.'

'Yes we will,' Holly said determinedly. 'Yes we jolly well will!'

The train roared past and the gates began to lift. As the girls set off again a familiar Range Rover pulled up beside them, honking its horn.

Holly turned. 'Dad!' she exclaimed.

In the back seat sat Jamie and Belinda. She leaned from the window. 'Quick!' she said. 'Your dad said he'll drop us off on his way to the sports centre.'

Holly's father got out and opened the tailgate of the Range Rover. He put the bikes in the back then got back into the driver's seat.

Holly thrust open the door and climbed in beside her father. Tracy clambered in the back.

'Did Belinda tell you why we were in such a hurry, Dad?'

Mr Adams shook his head. 'No, just that it was an emergency. What are you girls up to?'

Holly turned to glance at her friends. 'We'll tell you later, Dad. Please get a move on.'

'Holly, this is a fifty mile an hour limit. You don't want us to get done for speeding, do you?'

Holly wriggled impatiently in her seat. 'No, but please hurry, Dad!'

'What *are* you up to?' Jamie asked suspiciously. 'One of your mysteries, I bet.'

Holly tapped her nose. 'You'll find out in good

time,' she said. When Irma Stella was found out to be a liar and a blackmailer, *everyone* would know.

'I'm not sure where York Street is,' Mr Adams said.

'It's down near the canal,' Holly explained.

At the end of the street Holly said hurriedly. 'It's OK, Dad, you can drop us here.'

'Thanks, Mr Adams.' Tracy and Belinda jumped out.

'Are you going to be all right?' Mr Adams said, getting out and taking Holly's and Tracy's bicycles from the back. He looked concerned. 'How will you get back, Belinda?'

'Don't worry,' Belinda said hurriedly. 'I'll find a way.'

'OK,' Mr Adams said. 'I'll take your bike back with me. You can pick it up some other time.'

'Thanks.'

Holly and Tracy pedalled furiously towards the Stella-Howden offices, Belinda jogging alongside.

A green car was parked outside the building.

'That's the car Mr Benson rode off in,' Holly said, jumping off and propping her bicycle against the wall. 'That means they're still here.'

Holly went to push open the front door. When it refused to give way she rattled the handle impatiently. A desperate look crossed her face.

'It's locked!' she cried.

'How on earth did Mr Benson get in?' Tracy said.

'I don't know,' Holly grunted as she put her shoulder to the door and pushed as hard as she could. She shook her head. 'It's definitely locked. I suppose no one works here on a Saturday. Now what are we going to do?'

The girls stood a moment, catching their breath.

'What about that fire escape you told us about?' Belinda asked.

'Good thinking,' Tracy said. 'Come on, you two.'

She ran round the side of the building, the others at her heels.

'There's a door in this wall that goes into the courtyard,' Tracy said. 'There it is!'

They ran to the wooden door. Tracy rattled the handle. To their relief it opened. Tracy led the way.

The three girls stood at the bottom of the fire escape, looking up. The net curtain was still hanging from the kitchen window. Holly and Belinda looked doubtful.

'I don't fancy climbing up there,' Belinda said.

'You don't have to,' Tracy said quickly, one foot already on the bottom stair. 'I'll go round and let you in the front.'

The others held on to the rickety staircase to steady it whilst Tracy ran lightly up the iron steps.

'Be careful, Tracy,' Holly called anxiously as the staircase creaked and groaned.

But Tracy was already shinning up the knotted curtain. Holly and Belinda saw her grab hold of the window-sill and haul herself into the building. She leaned out.

'Go on!' she called impatiently. 'I'll meet you at the front entrance!'

In no time at all, Tracy had opened the front door and the girls were running up the stairs towards the Stella-Howden offices. As they reached the third floor landing, Holly put her arm out to hold Tracy and Belinda back. She held her fingers to her lips.

'Shh . . . listen!'

They could hear voices coming from inside. Two men were talking in hushed tones.

'Is it Mr Benson?' Tracy whispered.

'Sounds like it,' Belinda said.

'Well, there's only one way to find out,' Holly said in a determined voice. 'Let's go in and see!'

Mr Benson and his companion looked up in surprise when the girls appeared.

'Holly, Tracy, Belinda . . . ! What on earth are you doing here?'

But Holly and Tracy were staring at the man beside him.

'David!' Holly cried. 'How?'

David Benson smiled. 'So you're the girls who wrote to me. Well, it's good to meet you.'

'How . . . ' Holly began again.

David shook his head. 'There's no time to explain now. Let's just say when I got your letter I decided to find out what was going on.'

David turned to his father. 'I didn't tell you, Dad, because I didn't want to let on the girls had found out where I was. They wrote to me, told me what that woman was doing to you.'

'So that's why you came home. You said you had parole.'

'I do, on compassionate grounds.' David turned to the girls. 'The trouble is,' he said, 'I was supposed to report back early this morning. I'm already overdue by a couple of hours.'

'How did you get in here?' Belinda asked. 'The front door was locked.'

David smiled. 'I've still got a key. I worked here once.'

'But what are you doing here?' Mr Benson said to the girls with a puzzled frown. 'Is June all right? Has something happened?'

Holly quickly told the story.

The old man went pale and clutched the side of the desk for support. 'We'd better get back.'

'We've got to find something else printed on that faulty typewriter,' Holly said. 'Or something that will convince that driver he's making a big mistake.'

'And we've only got ten minutes left,' Belinda said, looking anxiously at her watch.

'A bit longer than that!' Tracy took something from the pocket of her jeans and held it up triumphantly. 'Look – I stole his ignition key!'

Holly and Belinda grinned. 'Great, Tracy!' Holly exclaimed.

'I suppose there might be a copy of those instructions somewhere,' David said, not sounding very hopeful. 'Although I hardly think she'd keep a copy of anything that would incriminate her. We've been looking for bank statements but haven't had any luck.'

'Bank statements?' Holly asked.

'Yes. I want to try to prove she took a large amount of money out of the company's account around the time I was supposed to have stolen it. Then at least I'll have some evidence the money disappeared while I was away.'

'Away?' Belinda said.

'Yes,' David continued grimly. 'I've never been able to prove it, that's the trouble.'

'Let's get a move on,' Mr Benson said. 'She could turn up here any minute.'

'We need to find evidence,' David said. 'And fast!'

14 *Confrontation*

At David's words, they began hurriedly looking through the filing cabinets.

'Everything's typed on the secretary's machine,' Tracy said angrily. 'We need something done on the old machine Mrs Stella keeps in her office. It's bound to be the one with the broken key. I'll just take a look in there. Keep an ear open, you two, just in case anyone comes.'

A few minutes later, Tracy emerged triumphant. She was waving a shorthand notepad and a couple of screwed-up sheets of paper.

'Look!' she said, taking a pencil from the secretary's desk. 'She's written something on here.' Tracy ran the pencil lightly over the pad. She held it up. 'See . . . it says "Road Widening Order" at the top. And I've typed out something on that old machine of hers. The letter "O" only prints in capitals!'

'What's this?' Belinda said suddenly. She tugged at a small green file hidden away at the very back of one of the filing cabinets. She opened it up.

'Hey!' she said. 'Look, David, copies of those letters she wrote to your parents . . . and a newspaper cutting. It's a report of your court case.'

'I wonder why she's kept that?' Holly remarked.

'To gloat, I expect,' David said bitterly.

'Let's have a look.' Tracy leaned over Belinda's shoulder. 'Hey,' she said, 'it says the theft of funds was reported on the fifteenth of August.'

'That's right,' David confirmed. 'She accused me of faking a business deal and forging a cheque. The cheque had been made out on the tenth of August. *Someone* forged my signature on it. You can guess who.'

'But you weren't here on that date.'

'I know. I was backpacking in Greece, but I had no witnesses to prove it.'

'But you *can* prove it, David,' Tracy said, her blue eyes shining with excitement.

David frowned. 'How?'

'The photograph . . . the one on the mantelpiece in your parents' sitting-room.'

David shook his head. 'I don't understand. I haven't been in the sitting-room since I got home.'

'It came through the post after you'd gone to prison,' Mr Benson explained. 'It just had an address on it, so we opened it. It was taken in Athens.'

'In Athens?'

'Yes,' Tracy said. 'You're standing in front of the Parthenon.'

David frowned, obviously trying to remember. Then his face cleared. 'Oh, yes, I remember. An American girl took it. I gave her my address but I never thought she'd send it. Well, well.'

'And . . . ' Tracy said excitedly, 'it's got the date imprinted on the bottom – the tenth of August. You know, some cameras do that. Print the date the photo was taken.'

'I haven't seen any date,' Mr Benson said.

'No.' Tracy looked a bit sheepish. 'It fell out of its mount when I picked it up. The printing was below the edge. I didn't think anything of it at the time.'

David grinned broadly. 'That's great!' He gave Tracy a hug. 'Now we're getting somewhere.'

'Why did Mrs Stella accuse you in the first place, David?' Belinda asked.

'She had a grudge against me. She was offering bribes to a district councillor, a friend of mine. She promised to pay him a large sum of money if he passed some building plans.'

'Why didn't he go to the police?'

David shrugged. 'She was blackmailing him too. Something about him being arrested for causing some trouble when he was a teenager . . . nothing very serious. Anyway, my pal knew he'd lose his job if his employer found out he had a police record. He'd got a wife and kids . . . ' David looked angry. 'That woman will stop at nothing,' he added bitterly. 'He told me what was going on and asked me to tell the police . . . Unfortunately I could never prove she was trying to bribe him. To get her own back, she set me up. And you know the rest of the story.'

Mr Benson looked suddenly alert. 'Shh!' he whispered. 'Someone's coming.'

Sure enough, Holly could hear the sound of footsteps coming up the stairs.

'Oh, no!' she exclaimed. 'I bet it's Mrs Stella. Quick, you lot, into the back office!'

The girls, Mr Benson and David hurried into the other room. They crouched beside the filing cabinets. Hardly daring to breathe, they heard someone enter the outer office, then go across to Irma Stella's room. The door opened, then shut with a bang. There was a click from the secretary's desktop switchboard as someone picked up a telephone and began to dial.

'I'm just going to try to see who it is,' Holly whispered. 'You four stay here. If I yell, come to my rescue!'

Keeping low, Holly crept into the secretary's office. She crouched down behind the desk. Beyond the frosted glass of Irma Stella's office door, a dark figure perched on the corner of her desk.

Holly stretched out her hand and quickly flipped

the intercom switch. Immediately, she heard the sound of heavy breathing and the quick, impatient tapping of long fingernails on a desk top.

Thinking quickly, Holly slid the secretary's drawer open. It was in there: Irma Stella's dictation machine! Thank goodness the secretary had picked it up from the repairers as she'd mentioned to Tracy. Holly placed it by the intercom, pressed the 'record' button and waited. A voice began to speak. There was no doubt in Holly's mind. It was Irma Stella!

There was a bitter laugh from the intercom.

'Yes . . . yes.' Holly heard her say. 'It arrived this morning. I expect by now their precious front garden will be ruined . . . I'll just say the driver made a mistake. Once the damage has been done, it'll be too late.' The laugh came again. 'These things do happen, you know.'

Hearing the woman's confession, it was all Holly could do to smother a gasp of anger.

'Look,' Irma Stella said. 'Thanks for lending me the van. You'd better dispose of that stuff in the back. Yes, yes, you'll get the money I promised you when the deal goes through. As long as you keep your mouth shut about what I've done, of course. Remember, you helped by getting that stuff for me . . . and the gun is licensed in your name. If anyone finds out, you're as much to blame as I am.'

Holly peeped over the top of the desk. Irma Stella was still perched with her back to the door.

The voice came over the intercom again.

'Yes, once the Bensons agree to sell me the land we can go ahead with the development. At least we'll be solvent again.' The voice laughed. 'Serves them right, stupid old . . . '

At these words, Holly heard a gasp behind her. Mr Benson was standing on the threshold of the inner office, brandishing his walking stick. His face was red with rage.

'Mr Benson!' Holly cried. 'Get down. She'll see you!'

But it was too late. Mr Benson had lurched forward.

'I'll get you!' he shouted. 'I very nearly gave in and sold the cottage to you. Scaring my wife . . . destroying my property. You wait!'

Mr Benson thrust open the office door. It landed with a resounding crash against the wall and the glass smashed into a thousand pieces. Ignoring the shattered fragments around his feet, the old man stumbled in, waving his walking stick threateningly. 'You wait . . . ' he shouted again.

Holly darted forward. 'Mr Benson!'

But David was too quick for her. He rushed in front and held his father's arm.

'Dad, it's no good!'

Irma Stella turned with a gasp. She was dressed in a dark jacket and trousers. Her long black hair was drawn severely back off her face. Her scarlet lips curled up in a sneer.

She narrowed her eyes when she saw David. 'What are *you* doing here! I thought you were still in prison.' Seeing the three girls behind the old man, Irma Stella's eyes widened in surprise, then narrowed again to a dark frown.

'What on earth?' she cried.

'We're here to find proof you're a liar,' David said angrily.

Irma Stella's dark eyes glittered as they rested on the file Holly clutched in her hand. 'And when I tell the police you've broken into my office and stolen confidential documents, we'll see who they believe,' she said coldly.

'Well, they won't believe you this time,' Holly blurted. 'We know you sent that digger to ruin the garden and we know you've been harassing the Bensons and threatening them with blackmail. You won't get away with it this time.' She waved the file in a gesture of defiance.

Suddenly Irma Stella dived round the other side of her desk and took something from the drawer. When she raised her hand, a small revolver gleamed in the light.

'Give me those papers,' Irma Stella said to Holly, holding out her other hand.

'Not likely,' Holly's pulse thudded with fear as she held the file behind her back.

'Don't be stupid,' Mrs Stella said icily, pointing the gun at Holly. 'Give them to me.'

'Do as she says, Holly,' David said in a low voice.

Reluctantly, Holly handed over the file.

'OK,' Irma Stella said, taking hold of Mr Benson's arm. 'I'll take the old man with me. If anyone follows me, I'll . . . '

'You wouldn't!' Belinda cried.

'Try me,' Irma Stella said, curling her lip in a sneer.

Pushing Mr Benson in front of her, she went out of the office.

'We can't just let her get away with it!' Tracy said angrily.

David shook his head. 'She'll do as she threatened. We'd better wait a while.'

Holly went to the dictation machine and took out the tape cassette.

'At least we've still got this,' she said with a sigh.

'Yes,' David said grimly. 'It's really all we need.'

'But we can't let her get away,' Tracy cried. 'We just can't!'

As she spoke, they heard the sound of a shot ringing up the stairs.

'Oh, my goodness!' David exclaimed.

Glancing at one another in horror, they rushed out of the office and down the stairs.

On the second floor landing, Mr Benson sat on the floor, looking dazed. He held Irma Stella's revolver in his hand.

'I managed to trip her up,' he said breathlessly. 'The gun went off as she dropped it.'

'Is she hurt?'

The old man shook his head. 'I don't think so. She went belting off . . . '

'If you hurry, you still might catch her.'

As they rushed down to the next floor there was the sound of a police siren outside, then a screech of brakes.

'The police!' Holly gasped. 'How on earth . . . ?'

A second later, a policeman came running up the stairs, two at a time.

'What's going on?' he asked. He looked at the three girls and David. Then at Mr Benson, who had stumbled down behind them. 'We've had a call from a neighbour of Mr Benson. Apparently his wife's worried about him. What's going on here?'

'Didn't you pass a woman on the stairs?' Holly asked quickly.

The police officer looked puzzled. 'No, I didn't pass anyone.'

The three members of the Mystery Club glanced at one another.

'I know,' Tracy said. 'I bet she heard the siren and went down the fire escape.'

'Quick, then!' Holly exclaimed. 'We should be able to head her off!'

Leaving David and his father to explain to the police officer, the girls ran to the kitchen along the corridor. They rushed to the window just in time to see Irma Stella jump from the fire escape and rush through the courtyard. She disappeared through the wooden door.

'Quick!' Holly cried. 'Out the front! We'll try to head her off.'

As they rushed out the front door the policeman called out. 'Come back, you three!'

But they were off, dashing towards the alleyway.

It was dark and dismal. Moisture dripped from the high brick walls on either side of the narrow passage. Empty drink cans and litter lay in the gulley.

'Hey,' Holly said suddenly, stopping briefly to pick something up. 'It's those papers! What on earth?'

Along the alley in front of them, sheets of paper fluttered along the edges of the walls.

'Why she's dropping them?' Belinda gasped, stooping to pick up several more.

'Probably to slow us down,' Tracy panted. 'Leave them, we can come back for them later. We can't let her get away!'

At the end of the alley, several cars were parked along the quay. The girls caught sight once again of Irma Stella. A man walking his dog narrowly avoided being mown down as she dashed past. She headed towards the quay wall. Several motor cruisers were moored about a hundred yards from the parked vehicles.

Holly pointed. 'There she is! She's heading for those boats.' She stopped suddenly, frowning.

'What's up?' Belinda gasped, stopping too. Her face was red with exertion, her glasses steamed up. 'I don't think I can run any more . . . ' She rested for a second or two, leaning over with her hands on her knees.

Holly set off again. 'I've just realised something. Come on, Belinda!'

'Oh, no!' Tracy gasped as Irma Stella suddenly stopped and unwound a rope from its mooring ring. They were only metres away now.

Reaching the edge, first, Tracy lunged forward. She grabbed hold of Irma Stella's dark jacket as she began to lower herself over the wall. She tugged with all her might.

'Help!' Tracy called to the others. She fell back heavily as the woman shrugged off the jacket and jumped into a small motor boat.

They stood watching helplessly as the engine gunned and Irma Stella sped away, the mooring rope trailing over the stern. Tracy threw the jacket down in disgust.

'She's got away!' she cried.

'What's this?' Belinda held up something that had fallen from the coat pocket. 'A balaclava!'

'I knew it!' Holly exclaimed. 'She's the one who's been doing all those rotten things. There's no one else doing her dirty work after all!'

'You mean the man at the Bensons' cottage wasn't a man at all?' Belinda said incredulously.

'That's right,' Holly said.

'Well, she's not getting away with it!' Tracy shouted. 'Look . . . she's heading for the lock. I bet I can get there first and shut the gates!'

With that she sped away, sprinting towards the lock as fast as her legs would carry her.

Before the others could set off after her, David and Mr Benson arrived in the police car. They jumped out.

'Look, Mr Benson,' Holly said, holding out the balaclava and jacket. 'The person who's been doing all those awful things to you was Irma Stella herself!'

Mr Benson looked at the articles in disbelief. He scratched his head. 'Well, I never . . . She's crazier than I thought!'

'Has she got away?' David asked quickly.

Holly pointed to the small craft disappearing upstream. 'Not yet. She's taken that boat, but

Tracy's going to try to close the lock gates before she gets there.'

'Let's go!' the police officer said.

David and the two girls clambered into the car.

They arrived just in time to see Tracy frantically winding the handle to close the lock gates. David jumped from the car to run and help. Below, Irma Stella, seeing the gates closing, quickly turned the boat to head back downstream. As she did so, the engine stalled. She pulled frantically at the starter.

'Oh, no, you don't,' Holly yelled. She dived into the water and swam strongly towards the motor boat. Grabbing hold of the mooring rope, she turned the craft and headed back towards the bank, towing the boat behind her.

Desperately, Irma Stella tried to wrench the rope away from Holly's hand. But when she saw the reception committee waiting on the bank she gave up and sat disconsolately in the stern.

Several pairs of arms leaned down to help Holly from the water. Tracy and Belinda ran to hug her.

'The water's freezing,' she said, shivering. 'You might have warned me!'

They stood and watched as another police car arrived to take Irma Stella away.

'When did you first realise it was Irma?' David

asked, as they drove at full speed back to Goldenwood Lane.

Holly snuggled beneath the red blanket the policeman had wrapped round her. 'I recognised the way she ran,' she explained. 'Then it just all seemed to fall into place,' she said. 'Why Belinda didn't see the van driver at Parkmead, only Mrs Stella in the window, for instance.'

'Yes, go on.' David said.

'And she had that plaster on her hand, remember?' Tracy said. 'Belinda said that person with the gun had fallen into the brambles.'

'You did a grand job, you three,' Mr Benson said gratefully. 'I don't know how June and I are going to thank you.'

'Let's just hope that digger driver hasn't got a spare key,' Holly said grimly. 'If he has, we could still be too late!'

But when they arrived, the digger was still standing idle by the front fence.

'Thank goodness for that!' Tracy exclaimed.

At the gate, Mrs Benson and the driver stood talking to a police officer.

'The officer said he'd radioed on ahead,' Mr Benson explained. 'The police station sent out a car to York Street to investigate.'

Standing near Mrs Benson was another man the girls recognised. The man with the binoculars who had been spying on the cottage!

'Come on, you three,' David said, holding the door open for them to climb out. 'I'm sure my mother will want to say thank you.'

Holly shook her head. 'I don't think it's over yet, David,' She pointed. 'That's the man we saw spying on the cottage!'

Mr Benson laughed. 'Oh, Holly,' he said, 'that's old George Pugh. He's a great birdwatcher. He's always on the lookout for rare species. He spends hours with those binoculars. If I'd have seen him myself, I could have told you that.'

The girls looked at one another and laughed.

'A birdwatcher!' Holly cried. 'Who would have guessed?'

Mr Pugh came over. 'I'm sorry about frightening your horse that day, young lady,' he said to Holly. 'I've been hoping to get the chance to apologise. I say, you look rather wet. Been swimming in your clothes?'

Holly grinned. 'Yes, although I don't think I'll make a habit of it.'

Just then a grey telephone company van drew up. A man got out and came over.

'There's something wrong with the wires,' he explained. 'That's why your phone's not working. It's been making loud humming noises, apparently . . . '

'He must have wondered why we all laughed,' Mrs

Benson said, pouring mugs of tea in the kitchen when the excitement had died down. 'I could hardly tell him I thought it was a ghost making the noise, now could I?'

'And you say Irma Stella dressed up in that old net curtain you found at her office?' Mr Benson said.

Holly nodded. She was sitting at the table wearing Mrs Benson's quilted dressing-gown while her clothes dried by the stove. 'Don't you remember? A scrap of it was caught between the floorboards.'

Belinda sighed. 'It's not nearly as exciting as a real ghost!'

'I'd sure like to take another look at that cellar,' Tracy said enthusiastically. 'Who knows what we'll find down there.'

David grinned. 'Another mystery for you girls to investigate. If you wait until my appeal's gone through, I'll help you. With all that incriminating evidence you've gathered and the tape of Irma's phone call, I'm sure I'll be out of prison in no time.'

'Wow! That would be great!' Holly said, laughing. '"The mystery of the Smythe family treasure." How about that for a title of an article for the school magazine!'

'Sounds terrific,' Belinda said, taking a huge bit of chocolate cake. 'Old Steffie Smith will go green with envy.'

'Right,' Holly said. 'Let's start looking right away!'

'No way!' Belinda spluttered. 'Whatever's in the cellar has been there for a hundred and fifty years. It can at least wait until we've finished our cake!'

DANGEROUS TRICKS

by Fiona Kelly

Holly, Belinda and Tracy are back in the fifth thrilling adventure in the Mystery Club series, published by Knight Books.

Here is the first chapter . . .

1 *Tracy's new friend*

'You don't think Tracy's been kidnapped, do you?' said Belinda.

'I wouldn't have thought so,' said Holly. She looked at her watch. 'She's only fifteen minutes late.'

It was a bright afternoon in the small Yorkshire town of Willow Dale. Holly Adams and her friend Belinda Hayes were standing on a corner. Opposite them, the multiplex cinema dominated the far side of the street. They were in the more modern outskirts of the town, far removed from its peaceful, unchanging centre.

They were waiting for Tracy Foster, the third member of the Mystery Club.

'I'm not hanging about here much longer,' said Belinda. 'Where's that girl got to?' She peered up and down the street from behind her wire-framed spectacles.

'We'll give her another five minutes,' said Holly.

'OK, but if she's not here by then, I'm off home,' threatened Belinda. 'I'm half-starved already.' She looked around for somewhere to sit down and, finding nothing, leaned heavily against the wall. 'I'm tired out,' she said.

'You're always tired,' said Holly. 'Anyway, you can't go home. We've been talking about visiting the library for an entire week now. Don't you want us to find something for the festival?'

The day of the annual Willow Dale Festival was approaching. It was to be Holly's first festival and she wanted to be properly involved in the festivities. Which was why she had suggested to her friends that they go to the library in search of information about old local customs. Holly thought they should come up with something different for the school to do this year.

'She's probably been waylaid by Kurt,' said Belinda. 'You know what those two are like when they get together.' Kurt Welford was Tracy's occasional boyfriend. Belinda thought boys were a waste of space. Holly didn't mind Kurt one way or the other – except when he made Tracy late.

'She's more likely to be showing everyone that report I did in the school magazine of her winning the tennis tournament,' said Holly. 'She said it was the best bit of writing I've done.'

'Only because it was about *her*,' said Belinda.

'Look!' said Holly. 'There she is.' Tracy and a boy had come out of a side road.

'And she's with Kurt,' said Belinda. 'What did I tell you?'

'That's not Kurt,' said Holly. 'You need new glasses.'

It certainly wasn't Kurt, as even Belinda could see now she looked properly. The boy with Tracy had black hair and Kurt's hair was blond. And he was shorter than Kurt, and thinner, with a narrow, sharp face.

'Who is it, then?'

'I don't know. Oh – yes I do. It's that new boy. What's his name? He's in the year above us. Mark something. I know: Mark Greenaway.'

'Him?' said Belinda, rolling her eyes. 'Trust Tracy.'

'What's that supposed to mean?' asked Holly. 'You don't even know him.' The Greenaways had been in Willow Dale for only a few weeks.

'His parents are absolutely potty,' said Belinda. 'Haven't you heard? My mum got it all through the local grapevine. She was telling me all about it the other evening.' Belinda's mother was a leading light in Willow Dale society, and it was important to her that she knew everything that was going on.

'Your mum is the world's worst gossip,' said Holly. 'I like to think I'm above that sort of thing.' Tracy caught sight of them and waved. Holly waved back. 'Quickly,' said Holly. 'Tell me *all* about it before they get here.'

'His mother is some sort of whacky faith healer,' Belinda began. 'And his father is a kind of magician or something. They've taken the lease on a shop in Radnor Street. Apparently they – oh, hello, Tracy. You're late.'

Tracy came bounding along the pavement, her blonde hair bouncing on her shoulders and her blue eyes sparkling. Mark Greenaway followed in her energetic wake.

'Hi, you guys. I want you to meet Mark,' said Tracy, her American accent more obvious than usual. She always sounded more American when she was excited. 'Mark, this is Holly. You two should have lots in common – Holly's from London, too. Mark's folks have just moved up from London, Holly.'

'The place must be almost empty,' said Belinda. 'Have they got the plague down there or something?'

'This is Belinda,' Tracy told Mark. 'Don't worry about her – she's always like this. These are my absolute best friends, Mark. You wouldn't believe the things we've gotten involved in since Holly showed up.'

'Tracy tells me you've set up a mystery club,' Mark said with a smile. 'It sounds interesting.'

'Interesting is hardly the word,' said Belinda.

'We do seem to get tangled up in some strange things,' said Holly. 'Only the other week – '

'Mark used to edit a school magazine in London,' interrupted Tracy. 'I've suggested he has a word with Steffie – perhaps he could write some stuff for our mag.' Steffie Smith was the editor of the school magazine. 'He could start up a magic column. You know loads of magic tricks, don't you, Mark?'

'A few,' said Mark. 'My parents perform at parties and things like that. I know a few simple tricks.'

'Don't be so modest,' said Tracy. 'Mark's got this great trick with a watch, haven't you, Mark? Go on – show them.'

'OK,' said Mark. 'If someone will lend me a wristwatch.'

'Don't look at me,' said Belinda. 'My watch cost a fortune. My mum would kill me if anything happened to it.'

Holly unclasped her wristwatch and handed it to Mark. 'What part of London are you from?' she asked.

'We had a place in Kensington,' said Mark, taking out a handkerchief and wrapping it around Holly's watch.

'Whereabouts in Kensington?' asked Holly. 'I might know it. We used to go shopping around there sometimes.'

'You wouldn't know it,' said Mark. 'It was just a little street round the back of Harrods. But then my parents decided they'd had enough of the rat race, so we ended up here. What brought you here?'

'My mum was offered managership of her own branch of the bank she works for,' said Holly. 'My dad was a solicitor, but he'd been wanting to give it up to concentrate on his carpentry work for ages – so Mum's transfer seemed the perfect opportunity. I felt a bit out of it to start off with, but this is a lovely place once you get used to it and make a few friends.'

'It's a bit dead, though, isn't it?' said Mark. 'Still, I suppose I'd better try and make the best of it. If my parents make a go of their shop we'll probably be stuck here for a while.'

'What do they sell?' asked Holly, preferring to ignore his uncomplimentary remarks about the town that she had grown to love.

'Oh – magic tricks, herbal remedies. Wholefood. You know – new age stuff. All sorts of things. You ought to take a look.'

'I can't wait,' Belinda said drily. 'We are really short of magic tricks and wholefood in this town.'

Mark laid the bundled handkerchief on the pavement. 'OK,' he said. 'Stand back while I say the magic words.'

They stepped backwards. Mark stretched his hands out. 'Hocus pocus, never fear – let the wrist-watch disappear,' he said solemnly. He looked round at them. 'That's it,' he said. 'It's gone.'

They looked down at the folded-up handkerchief.

'I bet it was never in there,' said Belinda. 'You've probably tucked it up your sleeve.'

'Search me if you like,' said Mark.

Holly bent to pick up the handkerchief.

'Just a second,' said Mark. He lifted his foot and stamped down heavily on the handkerchief. There was a disturbing crunching noise. Holly's jaw fell open.

'Oh, dear,' said Mark. 'It doesn't sound like it worked, does it?'

'My watch!' yelled Holly.

Mark crouched and gingerly unwrapped the handkerchief. Broken bits of watch were revealed. He looked up at Holly. 'I'm really sorry,' he said. 'It *usually* works.'

Holly was speechless.

Mark picked the handkerchief up. 'I'll pay for it. How much did it cost?'

'I don't know,' said Holly, aghast. 'My brother Jamie bought it for me for Christmas last year.'

Mark pulled a fat wallet out of his back pocket. 'I'll pay for a new one,' he said. 'It's the least I can do.'

'But it was a *present*,' said Holly. 'You can't just buy a new one as if . . . ' She stopped. Mark had opened the bulging wallet and had pulled out a wristwatch, holding it by the strap between finger and thumb.

Tracy burst out laughing.

'Will this one do instead?' asked Mark, waving the watch in front of Holly's eyes. It was her own wristwatch. Undamaged.

Belinda grinned. 'He had you going with that one, didn't he?' she said. 'I told you your watch was never in there. Not a bad trick. Not bad at all.'

Holly examined the watch. It was hers all right. 'How did you do that?' she asked.

'Magic,' said Mark.

Holly strapped her watch on, trying to join in with the general amusement, but feeling slightly annoyed that she had been taken in by his trick.

'Didn't I tell you he knows some good stuff?' said Tracy. 'Wasn't that great?'

'Very clever,' said Holly, frowning at Mark. 'You won't catch me out like *that* again.' Her face cleared. 'OK,' she said. 'It was good. You had me fooled.'

'He's got loads of other tricks,' said Tracy.

'The library will be closing in half an hour,' said Belinda. 'If we're still going there.'

'Hey, listen,' said Tracy. 'Do you guys mind if I take a rain check on that? Mark's invited me to the cinema. Why don't we all go see a movie instead? We can visit the library any old time.'

'I think I'll give it a miss,' said Holly. 'We keep putting the library off, and the festival is only two weeks away. If we don't think of something soon it'll be too late.'

'Oh, OK,' said Tracy. 'You two have a good time, then. I'll tell you all about the film tomorrow. Coming, Mark?'

They crossed the road, leaving Belinda and Holly gazing after them.

'Well,' said Belinda. 'She didn't waste any time. I wonder what Kurt will make of that?'

'She's just being friendly,' said Holly. 'You know what she's like. I expect he feels like I did when I first arrived. She's just taking him under her wing. It's a bit odd, though, him saying he lived in Kensington.'

'What's so odd about that?' asked Belinda. 'People do live there, don't they?'

'Yes, but he said they lived in a street round the back of Harrods. Harrods isn't in Kensington. It's in Knightsbridge, and it's an incredibly posh area. They'd have to be really rich to live somewhere like that.'

'Perhaps they are,' said Belinda.

'What? With a magician dad and a mother who does faith healing?' said Holly. 'I wouldn't have thought so.'

'Perhaps his dad's a really *famous* magician,' said Belinda. 'Or maybe Mark just made it up to try and impress us. Does it matter?'

'I suppose not,' said Holly. 'It's a bit odd, that's all. And I didn't like that comment he made about Willow Dale being dead.'

'He's only just got here,' said Belinda. 'Give him a chance.'

They headed towards the library.

'I think I saw how that trick was done,' said Belinda. 'Lend me your watch and I'll give it a try.'

'Not in a million years,' said Holly. 'I don't want your great hoof coming down on it. I nearly had a heart attack with Mark just then, and he knew what he was doing.'

The library was a modern building, part of the rash of newer houses and offices and shops that had been built around the quiet, old heart of the town. Inside, they went straight over to the desk with the computerised filing system. Belinda sat down, and started tapping the keyboard.

'Now, then,' said Belinda. 'What shall we look under?'

'F for folklore?' suggested Holly.

The visual display screen filled with green writing. 'Got it,' said Belinda. 'Right. Follow me.'

They gathered half a dozen heavy books from the shelves and took them over to the reading tables.

'This is perfect,' said Holly, as they started going through the books. 'There's lots of stuff here. We're bound to be able to come up with something.'

As they pored over the books Holly couldn't help overhearing a couple of women chatting at the next table. She didn't *listen*, but her natural inquisitiveness made it impossible for them not to gain her attention.

'That's two burglaries in the past fortnight,' said one of them. 'It's getting so you don't feel safe in your own home.'

'I know,' said the other. 'And they say that the burglars knew exactly what to take.'

'Well, I'm having window locks fitted,' said the first one. 'I know I haven't got a house full of antiques like they do over in Fitzwilliam Street – but you can't be too careful.'

'Did you hear that?' whispered Holly. 'Fitzwilliam Street – that's only round the corner from you.'

'I know all about it,' said Belinda. 'Mum's going round checking all the doors and windows every night. They'd have a field day in our place. Unless they went into my room, of course. Still, you never know. Perhaps they'd steal all those horrible expensive clothes my mum keeps trying to get me to wear. I wouldn't mind *that*.'

Despite her wealthy background, Belinda insisted on slopping around in jeans and an old green sweatshirt. Her only concession was her thoroughbred horse, which to her mother's despair, she had named Meltdown.

'Anyway,' said Belinda. 'Don't start trying to solve these burglaries. I've had more than enough excitement with you recently. Let's concentrate on finding something interesting for the festival, shall we?'

'I've got it,' said Holly. 'Look at this.'

She pointed to the open book. There was a column of writing and a drawing of a woman decked out in a huge, colourful costume and mask. '"The Carnival Queen,"' read Belinda over Holly's shoulder. '"In olden days a young girl from the local community was chosen to be queen of the carnival. She was led through the streets decked out in flowers, accompanied by a jester, and followed by other members of the community dressed as animals. They passed in procession through the streets of the town, and the carnival reached its climax in a sacred grove, where a bonfire was lit and where the revellers spent the night feasting and carousing."' Belinda looked round at Holly. 'I don't remember anything like that at our festivals before,' she said. 'It sounds like we could have a lot of fun with that.'

'We could have a carnival queen, couldn't we?' said Holly brightly. 'We could make the costumes at school. That would be brilliant. What do you think?'

'It sounds promising,' said Belinda. 'The school always has its own float in the procession. If we could convince them to do it as a carnival queen float it would be the best thing the school's done for years.'

'And my dad could help build the float,' said Holly. 'He's great at things like that. Do you think Tracy would be interested in joining in?'

'Interested?' said Belinda. 'She'll want to be the carnival queen if I know her. I can just see her in that costume.'

'We can take this idea to the school festival committee at the next meeting,' said Holly. 'The carnival queen will have to be chosen by the entire committee, but it wouldn't do any harm to suggest Tracy. She'd love it, wouldn't she? Standing up on a float in a fancy costume. Waving at everyone and being the centre of attention.' She gave Belinda a mischievous grin. 'Unless you fancy doing it, of course?'

'Very funny,' said Belinda. 'I'd rather die first. But I'll recommend you as the jester, if you like.'

'No thanks,' said Holly. 'I don't fancy performing. I'd rather just help out with putting the whole thing together.'

'Well, that's it, then, isn't it?' said Belinda. 'We'll tell Tracy all about it in the morning.' She put her hand to her ear. 'I can hear something,' she said. 'There's a tub of chocolate chip ice cream in the freezer at home – it's calling out for me to go and eat it. Coming?'

'You bet!' exclaimed Holly.

They caught the bus over to the better part of

town, where Belinda lived with her mother and father in their huge chalet-style house.

They were sitting eating ice cream at the kitchen table when Belinda's mother came in. She looked briefly in a mirror and patted her immaculate hair.

'Hello, Holly,' she said in her usual brisk way. 'Are you looking forward to our party?'

'What party?' asked Holly, looking at her friend.

'I forgot to mention it,' Belinda said glumly. 'Dad's going away to work in Brussels for a month. We're having a going-away party.' She gave a hollow grin. 'It'll be such fun.'

'It *will* be,' said her mother. She smiled at Holly. 'Anyone would think I was planning a trip to the dentist,' she said. 'I've told Belinda she can invite all her friends. And I've arranged a surprise.'

Belinda gave her a worried look. 'What sort of surprise?'

'You'll find out,' said her mother, sailing out of the room.

Belinda shook her head. 'I hope it *is* a surprise,' she said. 'Knowing my mother, it's more likely to be a shock.'

'Don't be such a misery,' said Holly. 'It might be fun.'

Belinda looked hollowly at her. 'It'll be dreadful,' she said. 'Take my word for it. It'll be absolutely dreadful.'

If you have enjoyed MISCHIEF AT MIDNIGHT, make sure you read Books 1, 2 and 3, and look out for further exciting titles in the Mystery Club series.

ISBN 0 340 60455 7